MISTLETOE in Park City

❧ CHRISTMAS IN THE CANYONS • BOOK THREE ❧

HOPE HOLLOWAY
AND
CECELIA SCOTT

Mistletoe in Park City

Christmas in the Canyons Book 3

Hope Holloway and Cecelia Scott

Christmas in the Canyons

Sleigh Bells in Park City
Snowfall in Park City
Mistletoe in Park City
Midnight in Park City

Chapter One

One Year Later

"Stop. Wait. Don't move."

At the urgency in her sister's voice, Cindy Kessler turned, gripping the bowl of cranberry sauce so it didn't slip out of her hands on the way to the table.

"Did you forget a garnish?" Cindy asked, lifting the bowl. "Because, like everything you make, MJ, this looks and smells divine."

"I forgot..." MJ sighed and brushed back some auburn hair, her blue eyes bright with...were those tears? "To say something to you."

Cindy eyed her suspiciously and gave a soft laugh. "You're about to get Thanksgiving Day mushy, aren't you? I'm going to get the big 'I love you more than anything' speech."

"Maybe. But give me two minutes..." MJ angled her head toward the bank of windows that looked out at the snow-capped mountains of Park City, Utah. "...before that old pine table our grandfather made is full of family and the conversation is loud. I want one private moment with you."

Cindy set the cranberry sauce on the brand-new quartz-topped island and took a few steps closer. "What is it, dear Mary Jane McBride?"

MJ chuckled at the name so few people ever used. "I just want to say that Snowberry Lodge isn't the only thing that transformed this year. You did, too."

"Oh." Cindy put her fingers on her lips as the compliment reached right down to her soul. "Thank you. I mean, I hope in a good way."

"In a *great* way, Cin. Think about where we were a year ago on Thanksgiving."

Cindy blew out a breath that fluttered her blond bangs, her mind slipping back to the dark days. A year ago, they didn't even know if they'd keep this lodge and the land that had been in the Starling family for generations. The fear of losing it had gripped her, stealing sleep and hope.

But then, everything changed in a way that sometimes Cindy still couldn't believe.

"That was a lifetime—and a million dollars—ago," Cindy said, her heart lifting at the thought. "Our whole world is...better, brighter, and bigger."

After the roof collapsed on New Year's Eve, they both thought nothing would ever be the same. And it wasn't, because that very night, the miracle had happened—in the form of a seven-figure gift from an unexpected source.

They immediately—well, after recovering from shock —launched a massive and daunting renovation, which included upgrading, improving, and remodeling this main lodge and all the cabins on the property. They weren't yet officially open for business, but they would start with a "soft reopening" first in the lodge, then the cabins, after Cindy's wedding in a few weeks.

"Well, this place has never looked better." MJ gazed lovingly at her massive country kitchen that now had commercial-grade appliances and custom-made cabinetry. "All this change—and Jack—has softened and relaxed you. Your skin is glowing, your eyes are bright—everything. You're beautiful."

The unexpected compliment pressed on Cindy's heart. Even for MJ, who was famously upbeat and optimistic, especially around the holidays, this felt like it was coming from somewhere deep.

"Thank you," she said again. "Jack sure made it easier to get through the days that seemed like one big filthy tarp and men in boots."

"So. Many. Tarps." MJ rolled her eyes. "And decisions."

They laughed, the number of decisions they'd made together having long ago become an inside joke.

"Look around, MJ. We kept the mountain magic of Snowberry. Every upgrade and remodel and addition feels as if it had been built by Owen Starling himself."

"Our grandfather would be proud of what we've done," MJ agreed. "But I think the change in you is more than our newly renovated lodge." She squeezed Cindy's hands. "You seem stronger and more grounded. You are about to start not only a whole new marriage—"

"With the same old guy," Cindy joked.

"With a *wonderful* guy," MJ corrected. "You are also starting a whole new career. And at sixty..."

Cindy winced at the number, but she held her sister's bright blue gaze, listening to every word that clearly came from her heart.

"I just want to say that I am so proud of you, Cindy Starling Kessler. And you are going to rock the wedding world."

Cindy sighed, holding back any quips because the moment was serious. "I'm excited about Snowberry Weddings," she said. "I know I should be stressing out about doing a job I've never done before—wedding planning!—but every time I walk into the Starling Room..."

She closed her eyes, picturing the stunning space they'd added, replacing the old mudroom and staff suite and extending into the yard. "I'm excited about the future. And we wouldn't have that room if not for you."

"If not for Matt Walker, you mean." MJ wrinkled her nose. "Sometimes I wonder if that interlude happened or I dreamed it."

"You most certainly did not dream it," Cindy said. "Just look around."

The proof that a kind and generous lottery winner had left them a million dollars—tax free and completely legal—was everywhere. But MJ didn't mean the money. She'd fallen for Matt, and he'd promised that he'd be back "in one year."

"Well, I haven't heard from him, so—"

"MJ, listen to me. Matt was clear in his letter to you—he wanted to spend a year giving away his fortune to people and causes who need it more than he does. Like us! He wrote that letter on New Year's Eve, so you still have more than a month before you doubt him."

"I know. You're right. And it's not like me to give up hope." MJ gave her an impulsive hug and when they pulled back, Cindy put a loving hand on her sister's cheek.

"You're glowing, too, you know," Cindy said. "You've covered your gray—"

"Gracie talked me into that. My daughter said I needed a bit of a refurbish myself." Laughing, MJ gave her a nudge when the oven timer dinged. "Now, go gather the troops. I'm getting the bird out of the oven and Benny likes to video the carving, which he will then put on TikTok because...Benny."

"Then let's do Thanksgiving!" Cindy pivoted and headed to the great room to call their family and friends for dinner, floating a little on the power of her sister's sweet words.

AN HOUR OR SO LATER, eleven people lingered around the table, laughing, talking, and—in the case of Cindy's father, Red—having thirds.

Cindy sat close to Jack Kessler, the man who held the

unique position of being her ex- *and* future husband. He hadn't been here for last year's Thanksgiving, but came a few days later...and never really left.

Last summer, they'd gone to Vermont together to sell his house—which they did with no problem. They also tried to persuade his eighty-six-year-old mother to move back to Park City, but failed. Although Bertie had agreed to come to their wedding.

For this whole year, Jack had been by Cindy's side. He'd rented a house just ten minutes away, and enthusiastically volunteered to assume all lodge management, freeing Cindy to run Snowberry Weddings, their newest venture.

It was no wonder MJ said she was glowing—Cindy had never been happier. Or busier, but that sat well on her workaholic shoulders.

"What are you thinking about?" Jack asked on a whisper, leaning into her. "Because you're smiling."

"Am I?" She touched her lips. "Well, I was just thinking about how happy I am."

He grinned at that, a glint in his dark eyes that gave her a thrill, even after twenty years of marriage, ten of divorce, and one second-chance year of engagement.

"Same," he said, coming closer to give her the lightest kiss. "I'm ready to start the sleigh rides, too."

MJ stopped all the conversations with a few taps of her fork against a wine glass. "Guess what time it is?" she asked in a teasing voice.

"We know the rules, Mom," Gracie said on a laugh.

"No one gets dessert until they say what they're grateful for this year."

"So let's do it fast!" Benny exclaimed from the bench he shared with Red. The two of them—one eleven, one eighty-three—had done an awful lot of muttering to each other during this dinner.

But that was to be expected. Benny and his great-grandfather had a bond unlike few others in the family. The combination of Red's old-man sarcasm and Benny's freakishly sharp brain was a match made in heaven—most of the time.

"You have somewhere to be?" MJ asked her grandson.

"Just..." Benny exchanged a look with Red.

"Newt's getting restless," Red said, clearly covering for him by drawing attention to Benny's dog, who was snoring at their feet and certainly not getting restless. In the year since Benny got the Cavapoo, the family finally had permission to shorten the dog's official name, so Sir Isaac Newton was now "Newt" and the light of Benny's life.

"How'd the octogenarian end up on a bench with the dog under him anyway?" Red mumbled.

"You insisted," Gracie reminded her grandfather. "So you and Benny could...what *are* you doing with that phone at the table?"

Benny shoved it under his leg. "Sorry," he said sheepishly, not looking sorry at all.

"Why don't we let our guests start?" Cindy held her

hand out to the four members of the Hale family, who would soon be extended family.

Cindy's daughter, Nicole, had gotten engaged to Cameron Hale last March on the top of a mountain on skis. Cindy and Jack couldn't be happier about the union, and they'd all become close friends with Cameron's parents and his extraordinary sister, Elise.

"I'll go first!" Elise leaned forward with her hands on the armrests of her wheelchair. A beautiful, vivacious twenty-five-year-old studying to be a vet, Elise had lost the use of her legs in a car accident many years ago.

She never let her handicap slow her down or dampen her infectious personality. "My gratitude list is long, starting with this girl right here." Elise gave Nicole's arm a squeeze.

"Hey, she's mine," Cameron joked.

"Sorry, Camelot. You must share this dear creature with me. It was Nicole who made sure I was able to start —and, may I add, *slay*—veterinary school." She gave Nicole a huge smile, but tears formed at the corners of her beautifully made-up eyes. "Because you believed in me, Nic, I'm living the dream."

"Aww." Nicole lifted the other woman's hand and gave it a sisterly squeeze. "I can't wait for you to be Dr. Hale."

Across the table, Nancy and Jim Hale watched the exchange with nothing but love in their eyes.

"I'm going to echo that," Nancy said, brushing back some hair as blond and wavy as her daughter's. "And I'm grateful to this man"—she smiled at her husband—"for finally giving in and agreeing to let Elise fly."

"Well, roll," Elise cracked. "How about you, Cam?"

"You stole my thunder," he said, pointing to Nicole. "I'm grateful for the most gorgeous and brilliant and supportive fiancée in the world and I can't wait to make this woman my wife."

Nicole angled her head and smiled with a happy sigh. "Thanks, babe," she mouthed.

"I'm also grateful that after I pass my boards in January, I will actually be a certified paramedic," he added.

That got a cheer around the table, everyone proud of Cameron's skills as a ski patrol at Deer Valley in the winter and a firefighter in the warmer months.

"How about my sister?" MJ asked. "What are you most grateful for, Cindy?"

"So many things I'm not sure where to start, but I'm going to climb on the Nicole wagon," she said.

Nicole groaned, briefly covering her face with her hands, her dark hair falling forward. "Too much attention on me."

"I'm grateful you got on a plane a year ago, flew to Vermont, and persuaded your father to come to Park City and run the Snowberry Sleigh. And win back my heart." Cindy lifted her left hand and let the diamond he'd given her moments before midnight last New Year's Eve catch the light. "I can't wait to be Mrs. Kessler...again."

There were more cheers and toasts for that.

"I'm grateful for a second chance," Jack said when

the commotion died down, his gaze on Cindy. "And the opportunity to run Snowberry, be with my family"—he glanced at Nicole—"and make up for lost time."

He leaned over and gave Cindy a sweet kiss on the temple just as she caught the rumble of Red's voice and the sharp whisper of Benny's—both of them looking at Red's phone screen.

"Really, you two?" she asked, pointing at them. "Texting at the table during MJ's gratitude game?"

"A text? Is that what this is?" Red asked Benny. "You called it...letters."

Benny ducked his head as if expecting to be reprimanded. "It's a TikTok DM," he explained. "And Grandpa doesn't know how to open it. Now, if I had my own phone—"

"Benny." Gracie gave her son a rare harsh look. "This is not the time for TikTok."

"But, Mom, I think this one's important."

Nancy and Jim appeared a little confused by the exchange.

"Benny started a very popular social media account last year called Grumpy Santa," Cindy explained.

"Oh, Nicole told us," Nancy said. "Are you running it again for this Christmas season, Benny?"

"Kind of," Benny said. "When Christmas ended, I morphed it into a Snowberry Lodge account then did some content on our renovations."

"*Some* content?" MJ asked on a laugh. "Benny made art out of the demolition, set 'before and after' videos to music, and interviewed the subcontractors like they were celebrities." You could hear the grandmotherly pride in her voice as she spoke.

"Impressive," Jim said, nodding to Benny.

"So what's the message, honey?" Gracie asked her son on a sigh. "And why is it important enough to discuss at the Thanksgiving table?"

Benny angled the screen and narrowed his eyes. "Looks like an influencer who goes by the handle of 'aisle files.'"

"*What?*" Cindy choked the word.

"It's aisle like A-I-S-L-E," he explained, misunderstanding her reaction. "That's a wedding thing, I guess."

The others laughed, but not Cindy or Nicole. They'd been buried in wedding research this year and knew exactly who this influencer was—and what she could do for Snowberry Weddings if they got on her radar.

"Aisle Files?" Nicole whispered, pressing her hands on the table like she had to contain herself. "What's the message? No, it doesn't matter. Whatever it is, the answer is yes. The right content from them could..." She looked at Cindy.

"Could book the Starling Room for a year," Cindy finished. "They have a massive YouTube channel with a million subscribers, a wedding planning podcast, and are famous for making a venue take off." She heard her voice rise with every word. "What did she say, Benny?"

"Oh, so now I can look at Grandpa's phone at the table?" he teased.

"Give that to me, honey." Gracie eased the device from his hand.

"Please, *someone* read it," Cindy said, trying to keep her voice steady.

Gracie sucked in a breath as she skimmed the note. "Brace yourself, Aunt Cindy. Dominique Parrish, owner of Aisle Files, says, 'Hello. We've been following your renovation and absolutely love the cozy mountain aesthetic, the family story, and—'"

"Of course she does," Jack murmured, squeezing Cindy's leg under the table, his excitement as real as hers.

"'—the heart your beautiful Starling Room will bring to small weddings. We heard that you have a ceremony planned on December tenth to debut the venue.'"

"How did she hear about our wedding?" Cindy rasped the question, still in disbelief.

Benny made a guilty face, and Red cocked a white brow. "Told you not to put that in a video."

"It's okay," Cindy said. "Keep reading, Gracie."

"'If so, we would love to feature the event with a small film crew and interviewer as part of our 'Intimate, Intentional, Incredible' winter series on spectacular venues. But we only do it as part of a wedding, not just a commercial. Think behind-the-scenes prep, ceremony details, and a short interview with the couple and venue team. No cost to you, full rights to use the footage, and we'll amplify across our channels with promos on YouTube, TikTok, and Instagram for a week before airing in January. Let me know if your bride and groom would be amenable and we can hop on a call this week.'"

For a moment, no one said a word until Cindy turned

to Jack. "Are we amenable?" she asked in a high-pitched whisper.

He just laughed. "I'm gonna say it looks like the guest list for our wedding just grew."

Cindy put her hand over her lips to keep from squealing. "And so did our gratitude list. Put Benny at the top! Honey, you are a rock star."

"And rock stars definitely have phones," he said. "Ahem, Mom, Christmas is around the corner."

Everyone talked at once, but Cindy sat in stone silence, trying to believe what just happened.

The break she needed, that's what. The launch pad that would catapult the Starling Room and Snowberry Weddings to massive success.

And it was her very own wedding that would make it happen!

"Are you sure?" she asked Jack as it all sank in. "It might...be a little distracting from the day."

"If you could see how happy you are right now"—he put his hand on her cheek, holding her face to his—"you wouldn't even ask."

She inched closer and kissed him right on the lips. "Thank you." Then she turned to Benny. "Please give her my name and number."

"I already did," Gracie said, handing Red's phone back.

Somehow, they got back to the gratitude lists, but through it all, Cindy felt like she might float to the ceiling.

Later, while they cleaned up, Gracie set out an array of desserts that proved why Sugarfall was the most popular bakery in Park City.

While everyone talked and laughed and nibbled the pumpkin tarts and apple pie, Cindy slipped around the corner of what used to be the mudroom, following a short hall to the double doors that opened into the back of the Starling Room.

Holding her breath, she turned the brass knob and stepped inside, chills dancing up her spine as she imagined Dominique Parrish seeing this room for the first time.

How could anyone not fall in love with this warm, inviting, extraordinary space?

The wide pine floor glowed golden in the waning daylight pouring in from a wall of French doors and huge windows. All that glass showcased a magnificent mountain view just beyond a brand-new gazebo built for summer weddings and private toasts. The white gazebo sat tucked into dark pines that glistened with new snow.

Cream silk drapes framed the windows in long, graceful lines, giving the room the perfect balance of elegance and coziness.

Her gaze lifted to the cathedral ceiling, its rough-hewn beams strong and proud, all holding bronze and glass chandeliers that spilled a gentle glow into the corners of the room.

But what pulled at her heart was the small, raised platform at the far end of what would be the "aisle" when the chairs were set up for weddings.

In the middle stood a wooden arch, big enough for a couple to stand under its curved canopy, its weathered frame more beautiful than anything polished and new.

No, the trellis—as they'd called it for decades—wasn't as perfect as the rest of the room, but Owen Starling had made that arch from the trees on this land for the occasion of his wedding to Irene in 1939.

To anyone with Starling blood, that trellis was perfect.

Cindy felt the weight of that history, of family and love layered into a room that so beautifully captured the old and new.

When Dominique saw this in person, she'd—

"Imagining your pitch?"

At the sound of Jack's voice behind her, she turned to see him leaning on the door jamb, arms crossed, a sweet smile on his handsome face.

"As a matter of fact..."

He chuckled, coming toward her, reaching for her hands. "Or are you thinking about our wedding?"

She heard the hopeful note in his voice, and it touched her. "I was admiring the trellis that you and Cameron literally packed into the UTV and hand-carried into this room." She chuckled at the memory of how determined Jack had been to transport the beast from what was once her grandmother's garden to this room. "I'm so glad you did that."

"I had to, Cin." He lifted one brow.

"Had to?" she asked.

He just shrugged. "Your family's history is important to me. It's what makes you...you."

She wrapped her arms around him. "You're so romantic, Jack."

"Hopeful and happy," he corrected, kissing her hair in a familiar move that always made her melt into him. "Not quite as happy as you are about this Dominique woman, though."

"It's exciting," she said. "We'll get advertising we could never afford and, honestly, that message just made all our lives easier. Not that I want it to complicate our special day."

"Then we won't let it," he said calmly. "And speaking of our day..." He pulled her a little closer, lifting his arm into a classic dance pose. "I've been thinking about our wedding dance," he admitted, swaying her a little.

As he started to move to music only he heard, she dropped her head on his shoulder, echoes of all the things MJ had said before dinner still in her head.

She *had* changed this past year, Cindy thought. Jack was a huge part of that change, too. He'd taken away a sense of loneliness, filling her life and her heart. He'd brought so much laughter to her days and peace to her nights.

And when he suggested taking over the lodge management, he'd given her a new professional purpose.

Instead of battling the spreadsheets that taunted her, instead of juggling vendors and payroll and reservations, she felt wildly creative and liberated by her new venture in weddings.

At sixty, she felt like her life was just starting, and that was truly the thing she was most grateful for on this snowy Thanksgiving evening.

Nothing could change that, just like nothing could tear Cindy and Jack Kessler apart again. She simply wouldn't let it.

Chapter Two

The thing about marshmallow frosting, Benny decided as he licked some from the top of a cupcake, was that it might as well be classified as an unstable molecular compound. Not technically, of course, because if you said that in front of a real chemist, they'd start asking for atomic weights and formulas and ruin the fun.

But in a practical, everyday sense, when you whip egg whites and sugar into stiff peaks, you create billions of tiny air bubbles trapped inside protein strands. That was chemistry. That was science.

So his mother didn't own a bakery as much as a lab, which was why Sugarfall was one of his favorite places on Earth.

And today, the Friday after Thanksgiving, it was even better because he was here with his best friend, the only person who'd want to work on a joint science project over a four-day weekend.

He took a look at that friend as he bit into the cupcake. Never in a million years would he have expected Olivia Hampton—the girl who beat him at last year's dog talent show, the girl whose dad opened a business that could take customers from Mom, the girl who showed up at school as the "new kid" and outscored him on the first science test—would be his closest friend.

But Olivia was the only kid his age who *got* him, who cared about school and winning things and figuring out the galaxy and doing hard math problems and playing chess like he did.

Which was precisely why the two of them had taken over the back corner table at Sugarfall. They'd stacked every inch with notebooks, diagrams, and a precarious tower of cookie samples to work on a science project that most kids wouldn't even think about until January.

Well, Benny McBride and Olivia Hampton weren't *most* kids and they both agreed that was just fine.

He chewed happily, comfortable with the smell of chocolate croissants and cinnamon rolls that wrapped around them like a sugary blanket in his mom's shop. Outside, snow drifted and all the tourists hustled by— some of them stopping to go into Craving Clean, the "anti-bakery" that Olivia's dad owned across the street.

"Our levitating cookie display is going to win the science fair," Benny declared, tapping his pencil against a page of complicated sketches. "Judges won't even know what hit them. It's revolutionary."

Across from him, Olivia twirled her pencil like a baton and stared at the snowy street. Her eyes got this glazed, sparkly look when she was daydreaming, like she was watching unicorns gallop through the clouds.

"Olivia," Benny said, not for the first time. "Focus. Your head's in the stratosphere today."

She blinked, then smiled in that mischievous way she always did when she was about to say something completely off topic, flipping back her braided hair.

"Do you think your mom and my dad would get married here in the bakery or over at the lodge?" she asked.

Benny dropped his pencil and didn't move when it rolled off the table, staring at her for dramatic impact.

"Olivia. Science fair. Not wedding fair."

"But it would be amazing," she whispered, leaning forward like they were plotting world domination. "Miss Gracie could be my stepmom. I'd get cake every single day. You'd get to hang out with Dad and learn all his football plays. It's literally the perfect equation."

Bending to retrieve the pencil, he dug deep for the same kind of patience Grandpa Red had to display when Benny cooked up a wild scheme. But this was not new information, and it was not in the realm of possibility.

Yes, he and Olivia had discussed this hypothesis months ago, when she made him watch one of the dumbest movies ever—*The Parent Trap*—and announced they had to get her father to marry his mother.

The problem? Their parents were mortal enemies and had been since the day Craving Clean opened and all the "healthy" people in town decided they'd rather have a coconut energy bite than a cream puff.

Well, they were nice enough to each other. But Benny, who'd perfected the art of eavesdropping, had heard Mom grumble plenty to people in the family about Marshall Hampton.

She was losing business to "health nuts" and it wasn't fair to compete with a former NFL player who was practically a celebrity. Plus, she whined that he made her whole body ache every time she looked at him.

He had no clue why his mom's cousin, Nicole, laughed so hard at that. Mom shouldn't ache!

"Look," Benny said, pointing to the page covered in arrows and magnetic field lines. "Magnetic levitation. Cookies floating in mid-air. We just need to stabilize the polarity so the chocolate chip doesn't crash into the oatmeal raisin. *That's* our plan for the experiment."

"Mistletoe," she answered.

"What? There's no mistletoe in magnetic levitation."

Her eyes, the same color as the night sky through his telescope, flashed. "Oh, but there might be, Benedict McBride. Because magnets are all about...attraction."

"You gotta lay off the ridiculous movies," he said, knowing he sounded more like his great-grandfather than a sixth grader.

"Benny! Mistletoe is for kissing."

He rolled his eyes so hard they probably went to the back of his skull. "Just forget about it," he said. "She's still mad about The Great Ashleigh Disaster."

Olivia cringed. "Yeah. That was bad. But my dad fired that marketing lady and he told your mom he was sorry she printed up those cards and put them all over town."

Cards that compared calories, ingredients, protein levels, sugar content—whoa, that was a big one—and seed oils? "She made everything in Sugarfall sound like poison."

"My dad thinks it is, but—"

"Which is why this...this *matchmaking*...is the dumbest thing a smart person ever suggested. Please, can we get back to work, Olivia?"

She sighed, biting her lip and ignoring him.

"Benny." She leaned in, her eyes holding him like one of those magnets. "Don't you want a dad?"

He swallowed. Of course he did. "I have one."

"And he's about as present and loving as my mother, which is basically zero and never."

She'd told him enough about her mom, who moved out to Los Angeles a while ago, to know that was true. Benny's dad, Sam Sutton, hadn't even shown up for his eleventh birthday in September.

"Well, I have Grandpa Red," he said.

"Who's a hundred."

He sniffed at the implication. "He's perfectly healthy and the greatest person who ever lived."

She held up her hand. "I know, I know. I like him a lot. In fact, I'd like him to be *my* great-grandfather, too, which he would be if..." She made her fingers walk and hummed that *Here Comes The Bride* song he'd heard Aunt Cindy hum.

"You're crazy," he said.

"You know I'm right."

He looked down at his notes, hating to admit how many times he'd had the same thought. Marshall Hampton was the coolest guy he knew. Once, he'd offered to teach Benny how to throw a football, which was something totally geeky brainiacs didn't get to do.

The bell over the bakery door jingled, and an older lady with gray hair pulled tightly off her face walked in, looking around before she smiled at Benny and waved.

"Who's that?" Olivia asked as the lady brushed some snowflakes from a bright red wool coat and walked toward them.

"Mrs. Locke," he said. "She basically runs everything in Park City. If she's here, she wants money, time, donations, or to hang a flyer in the window." When she reached them, he said, "Hi, Mrs. Locke."

"Hello, Benny. Did you have a nice Thanksgiving?"

"Yes, ma'am. Are you looking for my mom?"

"I am." She glanced past all the pastry displays to the kitchen. "Is she here?"

"She had to go into an emergency cake meeting with a customer, but I can give her a message for you."

She looked from him to Olivia, a smile growing. "You're such a nice young man, Benny. They just don't make them like you anymore. And who is your beautiful friend?"

"I'm Olivia Hampton." She straightened and held out her hand to shake Mrs. Locke's. "My dad and I moved here last year. He owns—"

"Craving Clean!" she exclaimed, shaking Olivia's hand. "I'm just on my way over there to talk to him."

"He's not there right now," Olivia said. "He took my dog to the vet for her checkup and shots." She made a face. "I didn't go because I can't stand it when Kat cries."

"You have a dog named Kat?" she asked, pulling out the third chair, so Benny grabbed his science book to let her sit down.

He was so used to people's reactions to Olivia's dog's name, he didn't even smile. Like his own pup, Sir Isaac Newton, Kat was named for a famous scientist, Katherine Johnson, so Benny had mad respect for that.

"It's a long story," Olivia said to the woman. "But I can give my dad a message for you, too."

"Awesome. I'm the coordinator for Park City's seasonal festivals," she said, "and I was hoping to speak with each of them about their gingerbread entries for the holiday festival."

"Oh, yeah," Benny said, remembering Mom had talked about that and how she didn't have time to bake and build such a thing, but had to.

"Do they both have to make one?" Olivia asked. "Because my dad's probably won't be, you know, regular gingerbread. Unless you don't mind almond flour and dried fruit instead of gumdrops."

"Whatever he wants to make." Mrs. Locke laid her clipboard on the table, eyeing their work. "The houses will be displayed along Main Street during Mistletoe on Main."

"Wait. What?" Olivia's big brown eyes grew to the size of chocolate cookies. "Did you say *mistletoe?*"

Oh, boy. Here she goes with the kissing again.

"It's our newest festival this year," the woman said excitedly. "We'll have an ice rink holiday extravaganza performance, all the snow globes that Park City is famous for, and every retailer up and down Main Street will display something festive—gingerbread houses, Santa's workshops, specially decorated trees, and, of course, mistletoe on every door."

"Of course," Olivia crooned, that goofy look in her eyes again.

"It's a little redundant on this block," Mrs. Locke said, making a squishy face. "Since these shops are both bakeries, I'm sure they'll both want to do gingerbread houses. I doubt either owner would prefer to do a tree."

"My mom might—"

"Maybe they could do one giant gingerbread house... *together*." Olivia slid Benny a look that was about as subtle as a space shuttle takeoff.

Together? Was she nuts? Yes, he recalled, she was nuts. About this.

"Oh, my. That would be..." Mrs. Locke frowned. "I really wanted one for every retailer."

Olivia narrowed her eyes at Benny as if she wanted support for this spectacularly bad idea. He offered none.

"I'd have to think about it," Mrs. Locke said. "And I have one more favor to ask, and this one is probably something you could help me with, Benny."

"Sure. What do you need?"

"The gentleman who is skating as Santa Claus with the troupe that's performing at the rink during Mistletoe on Main has thrown out his back. That's a problem, since we billed it as 'The Skating Spectacular with Santa,' so we must have one. I know Red Starling is the best Santa in town and he got so famous being Grumpy Santa last year."

Thanks to Benny and his insane social media skills.

"I need him to ice skate," she finished.

He almost laughed imagining how Red would feel about that. "He's kind of a sleigh Santa," Benny said. "I'm not so sure he'd get on ice skates."

"Of course, but all he'd have to do is push some toys across the ice, he wouldn't have to dance or anything." She pressed her hands together. "Would you ask him? We're desperate."

"How desperate?" Olivia asked.

The woman chuckled. "Well, we could find a Santa, but there's only one infamous Grumpy Santa! He put your lodge on the map."

Actually, Benny had done that, but he just nodded.

"We want the original Grumpy Santa, so would you test the waters—frozen as they may be—and see if he'd be interested?"

"I doubt he'd—"

"For a price," Olivia chimed in, making them both whip around to look at her. Now what was she up to?

"A price?" Mrs. Locke asked, fighting a smile. "Our troupe doesn't get paid."

"Oh, no money will exchange hands," she assured the woman. "But Benny's great-grandfather doesn't do favors for just anyone."

Her shoulders slumped.

"Except me," Benny added, knowing that if he wanted something bad enough, Red would move heaven and earth for him. But did he want this? He wasn't sure where Olivia was going.

"I have a, um, proposal for you," she said, leaning forward and looking a lot more like a future lawyer than a future scientist.

"A proposal?" The lady laughed.

"Benny will get you Grumpy Santa if you..." She slid a sideways look at Benny, who was lost, confused, and pretty sure that whatever she said next would cost him the phone he so desperately wanted for Christmas. "If you insist our parents make one gingerbread house together," she finished.

What?

Mrs. Locke drew back, blinking. "*I* insist?"

"Otherwise, they might not do it," Olivia added, "because it's so much work. But if they make one together, it's half the work and you get twice the house, and it will bridge the gap between these two businesses and be so good for Park City!"

Whoa, she could lay it on thick. Benny almost believed her. If she hadn't just been whining about *kissing* and *weddings*, he would believe her.

Mrs. Locke had to laugh. "You seem so determined..." She looked from one to the other again, her sharp eyes landing on Benny. "Why?"

"Because if they are so busy making gingerbread houses, then our Christmases will suffer," he said.

"And it will affect their businesses," Olivia added.

It actually made sense. "Why split the crowd when you could have one giant, amazing showpiece?" Benny said, catching the fever. "Less chaos, more wow factor."

She still didn't seem convinced.

"Plus," Olivia added smoothly, "think of the publicity. *Sugar Meets Clean: The Ultimate Gingerbread Collaboration.* Reporters will crawl all over it."

Gah, why didn't he think of that?

Mrs. Locke put her elbows on the table and gave them a look most kids only got from the principal at school, not that Benny had ever been called into that office.

"What's the *real* reason?" she asked.

Olivia sighed. "We're matchmaking," she admitted under her breath.

Wait. They were? And they were telling Mrs. Locke?

"We think they belong together," Olivia added.

Mrs. Locke's jaw dropped so hard it almost hit her chest. "You...they...match..." She gave a soft hoot. Then, she nodded. "Yes. You have a deal."

"Really?" Olivia looked like she might crawl over the table as they shook on the deal.

The older lady lifted her shoulder. "Please. I start watching Hallmark Christmas movies in August. I have a soft spot for a good romance. Get me Grumpy Santa and let your parents know they are co-creators of what I expect will be the biggest, most beautiful, most elaborate, and most unique Park City gingerbread house. Well done, future generation. You give me hope."

With that, she stood and walked out humming.

Somehow, they contained themselves but the second

the door jingled shut behind her, Olivia got up and actually danced across the black-and-white checkered floor.

"Operation Mistletoe Madness is officially a go," Olivia sang, slapping his hand for a high-five.

"Operation..." Oh, *man.* He was going to be in so much trouble.

But Olivia was his best friend. She was the only person he'd ever met who could solve a Rubik's Cube faster than he could and knew that mitochondrion was the singular of mitochondria.

And, he had to admit, her stupid idea might be really smart.

Chapter Three

Gracie

Gracie McBride set the tasting forks on the tray with a satisfied sigh. "So, we've landed on the chocolate espresso with the hazelnut cream, right? That will be the bottom tier. Then lemon with raspberry in the middle, and red velvet with vanilla bean at the top."

The bride, a petite brunette with a dazzling smile and nerves so frayed she trembled when she took a bite of cake, clutched her fiancé's arm.

"Yes, yes, that's it! Oh, my gosh, three cakes in one. I don't know why I panicked earlier about the lemon. This is perfect. It's *so* Christmas."

"Crisis averted," Gracie said, as relieved as the bride. These last-minute flavor freak-outs were part of the job, but they could throw off the kitchen. "Don't worry. You'll have a beautiful, delicious cake. Everything will be just right for your big day."

The groom, who had eaten more frosting than cake during the tasting, nodded emphatically. "This is the best cake I've ever had. She's not going to second-guess again."

The bride gave him a look that said, "Don't bet on it," but she was beaming again, so Gracie counted the session a win.

She walked them to the door, wrapping them in a light hug, feeling as much therapist as baker. "You're going to have the best cake and a beautiful wedding, I promise."

When the couple stepped outside, Gracie let her shoulders drop as she glanced around Sugarfall.

She had customers, yes. But no line out the door. No busy counter with a slew of staff bustling to fill orders. Just one person working today, and the tables were only half full.

Reluctantly, she glanced across the street to the green-and-white awning and crisp, contemporary lines of Craving Clean.

Oh, Marshall Hampton, how much I despise you and your healthy, pure, sugar-free, holier-than-thou, age-defying, energy-increasing, utterly guilt-free desserts.

No, she corrected her wayward thoughts. She didn't despise him. Just his competitive baking. The man himself she...

She gave a grunt and pushed the thought away. She never let herself go there except in her loneliest and most vulnerable moments. Otherwise, she was no better than a teenage girl nursing a debilitating crush on the single cutest guy she'd ever seen.

Because no matter how hard Marshall competed with her, no matter how much of her customer base he stole, no matter how he—and that pretty marketing guru named Ashleigh—worked to smear her products as toxic waste...she still got weak in the knees at the *thought* of the man.

Every darn time she caught sight of him—tall, fit, confident, with that easy smile that could melt glaciers—her brain short-circuited. She could barely string a sentence together. She avoided him whenever possible, because functioning in his presence was almost impossible.

Which was...pah-*thetic*.

"Hey, Mom."

At the sound of Benny's voice, she turned and smoothed her apron as she headed to the back of the shop where her son and the enemy's daughter had set up camp to work. Yes, she may have a love-hate war in her heart over Marshall, but Olivia?

Nothing but adoration for the kid who'd done what few others had ever succeeded at—she'd become Benny's good and trusted friend and had brought joy into their lives.

Gracie adored Olivia Hampton with her whole heart. She never got tired of seeing the two of them together.

"You are the only kids in America voluntarily doing schoolwork over Thanksgiving break," she teased, sliding into the chair that was already pulled out.

Benny playfully pointed the eraser side of his pencil in her direction. "It's not for school, Mom. It's for the Summit County Science Fair. Big difference. Huge competition. Cash prize. And we're going to win."

Gracie held up her hands in surrender. "Of course you are. I should've known better."

Olivia grinned. "We might come in second."

Benny choked and Olivia trilled a laugh. "I just say that to get a reaction from him."

Gracie chuckled at that. Olivia may match Benny IQ point-for-IQ point, but she had a whimsical sparkle and a dry wit that was purely irresistible. So that made both members of the Hampton family—father and daughter—irresistible.

She rested her chin on her hand. "So, what's the latest? Are we levitating cookies yet?"

Benny sighed. "Not yet. But we will. We just need to stabilize the polarity." He flipped a page in his notebook with authority.

"How was the wedding cake meeting?" Olivia asked.

"Long and full of second-guessing," Gracie answered. "Has it been busy out here?"

"Kinda. The events lady came by," Benny said. "For their festival thing."

"Eleanor Locke?" Gracie closed her eyes. "I knew she would."

"They're planning Mistletoe on Main," Olivia said, sounding far more enthusiastic than Benny.

"I know," Gracie said. "It's on my calendar for December sixth. I'm supposed to make a gingerbread house for that, aren't I?"

"Well," Benny said slowly, glancing at Olivia, "yes. You and—"

"My dad," Olivia cut in, sharing an unreadable look with Benny.

"He'll make one, too?" Of course he would, Gracie

thought. With granola and monk fruit and icing full of self-righteous healthiness.

"Actually, you're making it together," Olivia announced.

"Excuse me?"

"You know, like group projects in school," Benny said. "Only I bet Mr. Hampton won't miss a deadline and will be on time for every team meeting."

"Of course he will," Olivia said. "He's totally dependable like that, Miss Gracie."

Dependable and...gorgeous.

Gracie swallowed, unsure how she felt about this bombshell. Well, her stomach knew how it felt. Like it just got thrown down a rollercoaster and invaded by hummingbirds. And, of course, she felt blood rush to her cheeks like a billboard announcing her innermost feelings to the world.

Because no one blushed quite like a strawberry blond with freckles and a crush on the father of her son's best friend.

"I just don't know about this," she said, looking down.

"You're not still mad about the Snack Stats, are you?" Olivia asked, true concern in her eyes as she no doubt observed Gracie's pink cheeks.

"Oh, of course not," she said. "I *loved* having my ingredients plastered all over town and social media with actual devil faces next to my top-selling pastries."

Olivia bit her lip. "I'm sorry, Miss Gracie. So is my dad. He said Ashleigh Borrell will never darken his door again."

She laughed softly at the expression, suspecting those were Olivia's words, since she had a flair for the dramatic and a vocabulary that was lifted straight from Red's *New York Times* crossword puzzle.

"It's fine," she assured Olivia. "I'm just surprised we'd be paired, since our approach to baking is so different."

"Well, Mrs. Locke really only wanted one gingerbread house on this block, so you're doing it together," Benny said.

Gracie sighed. "That will be...challenging." Also thrilling and terrifying, and the blushing might actually give her a heart attack.

Olivia's eyes sparkled. "You can blend your styles."

How could they do that? First, she hated...chia seed sprinkles. Second, she melted like a truffle over a double boiler every time they were in the same room.

"My dad will be at the shop later today," Olivia told her. "You should go talk strategy or whatever."

"Yeah," Benny agreed. "The festival's soon, so you need to start planning now. That's how we approached our science project. You'll see, Mom. It'll be fun."

"And good for business," Olivia added. "Plus, you and Dad should..." She gave a meaningful look that Gracie took to mean they should be civil like normal adults who worked on the same street and whose kids were friends. Not *competitors*.

"I know," Gracie said. "Embrace our differences."

"Or each other," Olivia muttered. Gracie jerked backwards, not sure she'd heard right. "In the spirit of Christmas, of course," the little girl added.

Before she could respond, a small group of tourists walked in. "I'm going to run the counter for this rush. I'll talk to your dad," she added to Olivia. "Is he cool with this idea?"

"I don't know," she said. "Mrs. Locke was going to see him but he's out until this afternoon. So you better tell him."

"I will," she said with all the enthusiasm of a skydiver about to jump for the first time.

As she headed behind the counter, she thought about making a gingerbread house with the man who made her stomach swoop. A blush-fest, that's what it would be. He'd see through her crush in five minutes and...then what?

She dreaded the whole thing.

And kind of couldn't wait to get started.

Gracie stood on the sidewalk a little longer than necessary, rubbing her mittened hands together while she stepped back to take in the sight of Sugarfall bathed in golden afternoon light.

Her precious little bakery was so homey, from the leaded glass windows frosted with snow, to the glittering sign above the door, all the way to the adorable red mailbox for "Santa letters" that she put out every year in front of the shop.

Her bakery was the embodiment of downtown Park

City—quaint and historic, inviting and alive. Nestled beneath stunning mountain peaks, the old mining town never looked more beautiful than when it was covered in snow and holiday lights.

Turning to look across the street, she noticed how Craving Clean pulsed with an entirely different kind of energy, but still somehow fit in with Park City. A younger, healthier, more fit, and fantastic Park City.

Under the green-and-white awning, the glass storefront gleamed, spare and sleek and, well, clean. Everything about the place he so proudly described as the "anti-bakery" said discipline over decadence. It was hip where hers was sweet, crisp where hers was gooey, and pure where hers was...*poison.*

At least if you consulted one of the Snack Stats comparison cards that she hoped had all been trashed by now.

She crossed the street quickly, putting all that out of her head. There was room in this town for both of them, and she had to be the bigger person in all of this.

Pulling the heavy wooden door, she stepped inside Craving Clean, which was just as different from her place on the inside.

Where Sugarfall enveloped its customers in pleasure and nostalgia, Craving Clean projected precision. Fewer tables, all in straight, neat lines. A menu board with bold fonts, no flourishes. Every item—protein bites, oat bars, sugar-free truffles—was neatly displayed like an exhibit in a museum.

Of course, there was artfully placed Pittsburgh

Steelers memorabilia to draw the eye and impress the patrons.

And there were plenty of customers. Not a line out the door like when Craving Clean first opened, but quite a few people sipping smoothies in glass tumblers, biting into muffins the size of fists, nodding as if they were doing something good for their bodies.

Marshall Hampton was behind the counter, talking to a customer with that tall, broad-shouldered, effortless charm that made her toes curl in her boots.

When his gaze landed on her, his whole face lit.

"Gracie! Well, this is a treat. How's the science fair project going? I hope Olivia isn't eating you out of chocolate chip cookies. She doesn't get them here."

She came closer to the counter, praying her voice wasn't stretched thin or her cheeks weren't the color of those organic strawberry oatcakes in the display case.

"No, she's...she's just awesome," Gracie admitted. "I adore your daughter."

But not you, she thought quickly, praying nothing like that came out of her mouth. *I don't adore you. I really don't.*

"Well, the feeling's mutual," he said easily. "Olivia thinks you hung the very moon she hopes to visit one day."

Gracie laughed softly, rooting around for the perfect comeback, but she had nothing but a dry mouth and empty brain. No jokes about raising future astronauts or how Olivia's dog was named after a NASA scientist. No, all those witticisms would come to her around three o'clock in the morning when she mentally replayed this conversation.

"I, uh..." She cleared her throat. "I just wanted to stop by and, um, say your bakery looks...great. Really great. Very...clean."

He chuckled, leaning on the counter. "That's the idea."

Right. Of course. Clean. "And I wanted to tell you about a strange turn of events," she added.

He wiped his hands on a black apron and signaled to one of his staff. He had three people working today? Her heart dropped.

"Roberto, can you cover the counter? I'm going to grab a drink with Gracie."

He was? A drink?

"We have a great selection of tea." He gestured to the drink station. "Nettle and dandelion detox? Ashwagandha & Holy Basil Calm Brew?"

Oh, jeez. "Do you have coffee?"

"Great choice. Try it with hemp milk and monk fruit."

She just looked at him, trying not to react. From his laugh, she must have failed. "I have cream and..." He winked at her. "*You know what.* A small packet in the back."

She nearly melted like the very sugar he mocked. "Just black. Thank you."

He nodded and, a minute later, came out from behind the counter with two cups, leading her to an empty table—giving her hope that there was at least one of those. Maybe he wasn't stealing *all* the business.

"So," he said as they sat. "What brings you to the dark side?"

She laughed despite herself, letting the aroma of the coffee rise and give her inner strength.

"I've been over here before."

"Not very often," he said, breaking into a smile that... oh, goodness. Who needed sugar when his smile was so sweet?

"Well, it seems I might be here more frequently," she said, hoping to slide into the topic on her agenda and not just make small talk and gaze longingly into his impossibly dark eyes that were fringed with way too many long lashes.

Honestly, he was a beautiful man. His skin was the color of espresso dusted with cocoa powder, dark and warm. His hair was short, neat curls that framed his head, and he had just enough stubble to be masculine and not unshaven.

"I like the sound of that," he said.

The sound of...*what did she say?* She couldn't remember, since she'd been on another planet cataloging his perfection.

"Of you being here more often," he explained, the tiniest frown pulling. "Are you okay, Gracie?"

Good heavens, she had to get it together. "Yes, yes. I'm just the bearer of some surprising news."

A shadow of concern crossed his face. "Is Olivia

okay?" he asked, sitting up almost imperceptibly straighter.

She loved how much he cared for his daughter—it was evident anytime they were together. How she wished Sam felt that way about Benny. But her son's father was far away, physically and emotionally.

"She's fine, she's great." She felt her whole face light up. "She's a wonderful influence on Benny."

He beamed at the compliment. "That kid is special. And so's yours." He took a sip, holding her gaze over the rim. "So, what's up?"

She looked down at her cup and turned the handle to a right angle. "So, it seems we have to make a gingerbread house. Together, for the block. For the Mistletoe on Main festival."

Marshall straightened, brows raised. "Really? That's...interesting. Why only one?"

Gracie lifted her shoulders. "No idea. But the lady who's coordinating it stopped by and said that's what she wants. I guess they don't want two gingerbread houses on the same block. It's not bad marketing for us...for our shops."

He nodded, glancing around with a slight frown. "Guess we all could use a little marketing."

Really? Was he worried about the success of Craving Clean?

They regarded each other for a moment before he cocked his head. "Well, that's an interesting merger of... philosophies."

She smiled at the euphemism. "I have no idea how

we're supposed to blend our tastes in baked goods. You'll want to build walls out of flaxseed crackers, and I'll want mine to be made of, you know, *gingerbread.*"

"And you'll want frosting so sweet it could knock out a moose," he teased, "while I'll be looking for a zero-calorie cream substitute."

She wrinkled her nose. "That's not even food."

He grinned, and it made her insides flutter dangerously. "We'll find common ground."

Roberto came to the table then, carrying two plates.

"Just out of the oven, Marshall," the young man said. "I thought you'd like to treat your guest to your newest invention."

"That's awesome, Roberto. Thank you."

The man placed two plates on the table.

Gracie stared at two beautiful pastries with golden flaky crust and a pile of white froth and sucked in a breath. "Is that a cream puff?"

It looked a lot like her signature pastry, the very delectable dessert that had put Sugarfall on the map.

"I call it a Clean Puff," he said proudly. "The shell is made from almond flour and oat fiber, bound with egg whites and a touch of coconut oil."

Seriously? "Or you could use butter, flour, and egg yolks for a *pâte à choux* that would bring you to tears," she countered.

"Tears when I think about gut inflammation."

She felt her shoulders drop. "I don't think about things like that," she confessed.

He chuckled. "Anyway, the filling is a protein cream

made from a silken tofu base with vanilla plant protein and some natural sweeteners. On top is seventy percent cacao for chocolate, and a dusting of coconut. Go ahead, try it. I can give you the calories, fat, and sugar content, if you like."

"I'll pass on that, but not this." She picked up a small dessert fork and took a taste. The first bite was… "Darn you, Marshall Hampton."

"That's all you have to say?"

"Also, I hate you."

He laughed heartily. "Now, there's the high praise I wanted from you."

He wanted…praise from her?

She thanked him by taking another bite and closed her eyes. To a completely untrained and casual palate? It was perfection. Guilt-free and maddeningly satisfying.

"What do you think?" he asked. "I really want the opinion of a real pastry chef."

"My opinion is…" She swallowed a delicious bite. "Please don't hire that…that woman again to do a media blitz comparing my cream puffs to your Clean Puffs, because it will be game over." She dabbed her lips with a napkin. "For me."

His whole expression softened. "Hey, really, I'm so sorry about that card thing. That whole approach was a mistake. I don't want people not to go to your bakery! I just want more to come to mine."

So they were both feeling the pinch of competition. Gracie filed that and sipped her coffee. "Anyway, we do have to find that common ground for the good of our little community."

"Agreed." He braced his elbows on the table and leaned in. "What are you picturing for a gingerbread house?"

Gracie lifted her chin. "Well, gingerbread, for one thing. Actual gingerbread. With molasses, butter, eggs, flour. You know—ingredients that make people happy."

He rolled his eyes. "And spike their insulin like a ski jump. Got it."

"And lots of frosting," she powered on. "I envision some snowy rooflines and icicle fondant dripping down the eaves. Gumdrop paths. It should look like the North Pole and smell like Christmas."

Marshall nodded slowly, as though taking notes in his head. "Okay. Classic. Traditional. Sugary."

"Yes." She crossed her arms, bracing herself for his rebuttal, a little surprised at how relaxed she felt. Must be the...plant protein.

He rubbed his jaw. "See, I was thinking more... modern. Straight lines from almond flour panels instead of gingerbread so it holds longer. We could do windows made of isomalt."

She winced at the mention of the sugar-free substitute, even though it was known for making great "glass" on baked goods.

"Maybe a roof tiled with protein crisps," he finished.

She stared at him. "Protein crisps. On a gingerbread roof."

"Don't knock it till you try it," he said with a grin. "They're surprisingly architectural."

Despite herself, she laughed, and the sound startled her. He made it too easy. Too...fun.

She shook her head quickly and tried to steer the conversation back. "Look, whatever we build, it has to wow the town. This isn't just about your shop or mine. Mistletoe on Main is going to bring tourists, foot traffic, and oodles of attention. The better the gingerbread house, the better the turnout—for both of us."

Marshall nodded, that warm smile still lighting his face. "Exactly. And you know, it might be fun to sort of... show off our differences."

"I actually think that has potential," she said. "Let's go big in size, scale, scope...and our competitive edge."

"Okay. How?"

"Forget a house, let's do a gingerbread bakery," she said as a mental image took shape. "Two doors, two entrances. Maybe two buildings we creatively connect. One with your green-and-white awning and the Craving Clean logo. The other with my wooden sign and frost-encrusted windows. Big, maybe two feet tall. Side by side but...different doors."

For the first time, Marshall didn't immediately tease. His eyes sparked with something like admiration. "Well, now I see where your genius son gets his brains. That is a stinking brilliant idea, Gracie."

And...of course, she blushed. A gusher that no doubt painted her cheeks scarlet. She tried to ignore it and cleared her throat.

"So...uh, you'll get your protein shingles, and I'll get my gumdrops. One side modern, one side classic. It could work."

"It could," he agreed. "It could be amazing."

And for one breathless moment, she let herself picture it—not just the gingerbread house, but the two of them working on it.

Marshall with his sleeves rolled up, her with a piping bag in hand, standing close enough that she could smell that maddening mix of vanilla and clean soap that seemed to cling to him.

She shoved the thought away before she melted like his seventy percent cacao topping.

"My kitchen or yours?" he asked, yanking her back to reality with the question.

"Mine's bigger, but you'll surely get sugar shock just by walking in."

"I'll wear my armor," he said. "Yours *is* bigger and I'll do a lot of my work ahead of time. What day is this event?"

"The sixth and my calendar is crazy, but I'll make it work."

By the time she left, after more brainstorming, banter, and a schedule they could both meet, she realized she'd completely forgotten to be nervous around him.

She also forgot that she hated him. On the contrary, she liked him even more.

It was going to be a long gingerbread season this year, that was for sure. Long and not...horrible. Not horrible at all.

Chapter Four

Cindy

"Okay, Cindy, honey, walk me around." Dominique Parrish had a warm voice, but she spoke rapid-fire, like Cindy imagined everyone in New York did, forcing a person to really have to concentrate to follow. "Give me the full fantasy."

Cindy raised her phone so the camera could capture the view on the FaceTime call. This was her big chance to wow the woman who owned Aisle Files, and Cindy wanted to seize the moment.

They'd exchanged some small talk and Dominique reiterated what she was trying to accomplish with this feature, then Cindy took the phone into the Starling Room for a virtual tour.

She hoped it looked as good on a three-inch screen as it did in real life.

"I'll start with the view because it's second to none," Cindy said, turning her phone toward the bank of glass to her right. "This row of French doors lines one side of the room, with tall windows above and on each end to bring in more light. Just look at those mountains!"

"Pretty."

Pretty? That vista was breathtaking! Cindy tried to balance her phone in both hands, her own screen glowing with the cheerful, perfectly made-up face of a woman in her mid-forties with a striking appearance that the camera surely loved.

But all that mattered was that the camera loved the view, so Cindy zoomed in.

Outside, the November twilight slanted across the mountain peaks, painting the snow-dusted ridges in brushstrokes of lavender and rose. She'd timed the call to get this moment, and prayed the woman appreciated what she and MJ often called "pink mountains."

"Are you able to see how beautiful that is?" Cindy asked.

"It looks...wintry."

Cindy laughed. "It is now. In the spring, the snow will melt, and the summer is prettier still. But come October? The colors will blow your mind. We planned this room, and the lawn outside, for year-round weddings."

"Let's see the inside space," Dominique said.

"Of course." She began to walk the length of the room.

"The Starling Room is named for my family," she started, remembering the little speech Nicole had helped her prepare, bringing all her marketing education to the process. "My grandfather, Owen Starling, built this lodge when Park City began to change from a mining town to a ski and summer sport town."

"Mmm." Dominique frowned. "Max capacity?"

"Fifty, tops," she said, hoping that wasn't a ding. "My daughter's fiancé is a firefighter, so he helped us design a space that meets code for—"

"We don't want a big space for this feature," the other woman interjected, clearly not the least bit interested in fire codes. "We do a million of those three-hundred-people spaces. This piece will showcase intimate and intentional, and we want just that. Small weddings are all the rage and it's hard to find the right spot. What's the configuration for ceremony and reception?"

"This room is designed for both," Cindy explained, scanning the space with her phone camera. "The guests are seated here in the center area with the mountains in full view for the ceremony, with this as our aisle. When the vows are finished, guests are guided into our lodge dining space for cocktails and apps while the wedding staff flips the Starling Room for dinner and dancing."

"Oh, I love that. Ambitious, though."

Was it ever. "We're going for the intimacy of a family party with the elegance of a catered, lavish wedding."

Dominique let out a delighted squeal. "That's what I'm talking about. So many brides are looking for this, and I love the one-stop space and seamless transitions. That is *everything* right now. Saves money, saves time, saves stress."

Well, not for the owners, but relief poured through Cindy, boosting her confidence.

"That's what we thought when we designed it. Plus, Snowberry Weddings is meant to be turn-key. A bride can have it all here—ceremony, cocktail hour, reception, cake, music. One place, one vision. And we have the accommodations to sleep around thirty people in a newly renovated historic lodge with eight guest suites, plus six cabins on the property."

"Perfect."

Cindy angled the phone to show the ceiling, the chandeliers, the beams above that gave rustic weight to the elegance. Dominique seemed impressed, but far more interested in florals or lighting schemes. Cindy nodded, jotting mental notes, her excitement growing with every word.

"And what about this debut event that's happening?" Dominique asked finally. "Please tell me it's not going to be an uptight bridezilla who can't handle a little camera crew in her face."

Cindy laughed, dropping down to one of the chairs and touching the screen to flip the camera to herself. "You're looking at her."

"You?" She looked suitably surprised.

"Yes, I'm the sixty-year-old bride."

"Holy Golden Bachelorette! Tell me you are not lying right now."

"I'm not lying," Cindy assured her. "The fact is, I'm the first bride in this venue. I didn't build it for my own wedding, but...that's how it happened."

"Did you meet him on the apps?" Dominique asked, sounding deeply interested.

"Actually..." Cindy gave a very self-conscious laugh.

"I met him long before online dating existed. Jack and I were first married thirty years ago, then we divorced ten years . Last Christmas, my daughter convinced him to come here and help run our sleigh rides and...we fell back in love."

Dominique stared at her through the screen, her slightly over-filled lips in a perfect O shape. Then, she said, "I. Am. Dead."

Cindy cracked up at the reaction. "It's been quite a story."

"No, seriously, shut up! You had me at sleigh rides. Please tell me there's going to be one at your wedding. You're arriving by sleigh, Cindy, there's just no other way."

"I could do that," she said.

"So, let me get this straight. You're remarrying your husband at sixty, your daughter is the matchmaker, and you built the stinking venue on the family property? Am I missing anything else fantastic in this second-chance fairy tale?"

"Um...my husband was an Olympic skier and is quite good-looking."

"Of course he is!" she gushed. "You, my friend, are social media gold! And I'm mining for every nugget. Yes, yes, and yes!"

A giggle of joy rose up in Cindy. "That's awesome."

"Oh, honey, we rode our sleigh right past awesome a while ago. My followers are going to eat this up with a fork and spoon and come back for seconds and thirds.

You are the epitome of an Aisle Files bride, and I love everything about this event. And so will they!"

Cindy smiled so broadly it hurt her cheeks. "I'm so glad. I don't want the story to be about me, though. This is about the Starling—"

"The bride is the heart of every feature I do, even the ones that are about a venue like this. I'm so excited I could cry. Hashtag secondchances, hashtag happilyever-after, hashtag remarriedinstyle. Where will you walk the aisle? Take me through it again."

Cindy flipped the camera down the length of the room, pacing slowly so Dominique could imagine herself in the bride's place.

"Right here. We'll set chairs in two blocks with this center aisle. Flowers are winter green and white, with pops of red because it will be two weeks before Christmas."

Dominique was murmuring, "Oh, my gosh, I'm in love."

Cindy reached the raised stage and lifted the phone, smiling with pride. "And here is where we'll say our vows."

There was a pause. "Wait. What is that monstrosity?"

Cindy laughed, pretty sure what Dominique meant. The trellis loomed large, weathered and worn, solid oak and handmade joints.

"It'll look better with flowers," Cindy assured her.

"It will look better in a bonfire."

Cindy swayed a little at the heartless comment. She

took a deep breath and a step closer, determined to defend the piece of family history.

"Well, to be perfectly honest, it's a wedding arch, carved by my grandfather Owen in 1939 as his gift to his bride, my grandmother, Irene. Every Starling couple since has married under it." Everyone except her, but she left that out. "My fiancé, Jack, hauled it in here just last month so we could resume the tradition for our wedding."

Dominique pursed her glossy lips. "Oh, honey. It's gotta go."

Cindy blinked, then laughed. "It's not going anywhere."

"It's...quaint," Dominique allowed, her tone dipped in honey but edged with steel. "But it's an atrocity. Even with that cute family backstory, this is not going to fly in the viral world. You want to capture hearts *and* clicks? You need chic. Symmetry. Florals that explode on Instagram. That thing looks like it belongs in somebody's great-grandmother's garden."

This time, Cindy's laugh grew nervous. "Well, it *was* in my grandmother's garden. We brought it in."

"Then put it back, Cindy." Dominique softened her smile, but her head still shook. "Romance, big views, heart-tugging second chances? Yes, please. But something that looks like it was cut by Daniel Boone and nibbled by the local deer? Nope. We'll pass."

Pass? Her heart dropped. "You mean...you're not coming?"

"Yes, we're coming, but that thing is going. You can

bring it back afterwards if you like, but trust me on this, brides won't want it. Every one of them will demand you move it."

"We'll cover it in flowers."

"Nostalgia is not a trend. Trust me."

Cindy's hand tightened on the phone. "It means something to us. To our family."

"Of course it does," Dominique said smoothly. "But this is business, darling. You're launching a wedding brand, not a genealogy tour. Other than that, the room is perfection."

Cindy forced a nod, even as her stomach turned. "All right. I...see what you mean."

Dominique looked down at some notes, already moving on. "Perfect. Now, let's talk logistics. My team will arrive a few days before the wedding."

"Will you need accommodations?"

"No, we'll take care of all that. We'll put you out plenty, don't worry. Let me see, what else..."

Cindy grabbed her own notebook, scribbling as Dominique rattled through details. Instagram lives, bridal interviews, drone shots.

By the time the influencer wound down, Cindy felt both exhilarated and utterly out of her depth.

"So happy to talk to you, Cindy," Dominique said, blowing a kiss to the camera. "Second chances never looked so intimate, intentional, or incredible. This could blow up."

As long as it didn't blow up...in her face. "Okay. Great."

"I'll be in touch."

The screen went dark.

Cindy lowered the phone and walked slowly toward the trellis. The old, curved wood seemed to sag under Dominique's verdict, though Cindy knew it was as strong as the day Owen built it. She brushed her hand over the carved initials, tracing the grooves of O + I, the year 1939 etched forever.

Her throat tightened. It wasn't perfect, no—but it was *theirs*. It carried love, history, family. Every vow spoken here would be stronger for it.

And yet Dominique was right: to outsiders, it wasn't beautiful. To a bride scrolling Instagram, it might even look shabby.

Cindy's heart twisted and she dialed her daughter's number. She needed someone to talk to, and something told her Jack wasn't the one for this conversation. He'd tell Dominique "Your Arch Is Shabby" Parrish to take a hike right over a cliff.

And Cindy still wanted Aisle Files to happen. Only just a tiny bit less now.

CINDY PACED a slow figure eight up and down an imaginary aisle, pausing at the raised platform to stare at the trellis. With every step, she replayed Dominique's comments all bright and sure, telling her all the things to do and one thing to undo.

"Here I am!" The door opened with a quick whoosh and Nicole bounced in, cheeks pink from the chill, a knit cap shoved into her jacket pocket so her midnight locks fell over her shoulder. "Ski Shed just closed up, so I'm all yours. Didn't you have your call with Dominique?"

"Yes." Cindy dropped back on the same chair she'd been on before. "It went well. She's...wow. Quite a force."

"I know," Nicole said, moving around the room like a producer scouting a set. "I deep-dive stalked her while you were on the phone. We knew she was a big influencer, but this lady basically *owns* the wedding internet. Mom, this is a *big* deal."

"I know," Cindy said softly. "And she loved the Starling Room and loved my story with Dad even more."

"I knew it!" Nicole gave a clap and sat in one of the other chairs, shouldering out of her coat. "It's the stuff dreams are made of."

Cindy laughed lightly. "She also loved the one-stop shop concept. Ceremony here, then cocktail hour while we flip the room, then reception and dance floor with the band tucked over there." She pointed, and Nicole followed her finger with a satisfied nod. "She said it's all the rage. Her followers want pretty *and* practical."

"Well, I certainly do," Nicole agreed, no doubt thinking of her own wedding taking place on New Year's Eve in this very room. "Okay, what else? What trends? What shots? Tell me everything she wants to do."

Cindy launched into it, the ideas spilling as she remembered them all. "She talked about TikTok transitions—like a before-and-after flip of the room. A slow walk down the aisle with trending audio. Behind-the-scenes reels: me with the florist, you with the lighting guy, Jack checking out the sleigh rides outside. Maybe a quick interview about second chances."

Nicole's grin got huge. "This is perfect. This is exactly the kind of kickstart Snowberry Weddings needs. What a coup!"

Cindy pressed her fingertips to her lips as if she could keep in the bad part. "There was just...one weird thing."

Nicole's eyebrows shot up. "What?"

Cindy hesitated, then stood and walked to the platform, climbing up to where the trellis stood. She put a hand on it, trying to forget how Dominique had viciously described it. She wouldn't share that with Nicole—then she and Cameron wouldn't want to get married under it.

"She said this has to go. She said it's, um, not...Instagram worthy."

Nicole's mouth rounded. "Oof."

"She was pretty insistent," Cindy said, hearing the disappointment in her own voice. "In fact, it wasn't really up for discussion. She said sentimental things don't make for good social media. People want picture-perfect Instagram, not some old family wooden thing that means nothing to anyone who isn't a Starling."

Nicole winced in sympathy. "Well, I want it at my wedding, but then, I'm from Starling blood. I guess I get it. The vibe in here is so ethereal—those drapes, the light, the beams—and the trellis is...well, it's rustic in a way that doesn't photograph as high-end unless you style the heck out of it." She shrugged and stood, walking to the platform. "So we move it."

Cindy bit her lip. "I don't..." She sighed. "I think your dad is going to be disappointed. He really has so much respect for Starling family history."

She considered that, nodding and squinting at the trellis. "What about a compromise?"

"Such as?"

"We soften it," Nicole said, stepping closer to the platform. "We keep the structure—don't move it, don't hide it—but we dress it in a way that fits the Starling Room's look. Beautiful white drapery, maybe asymmetrical, with winter greens and a little sparkle. You still see the shape and feel the history, but your eye reads 'romantic arch,' not 'backyard arbor.'"

"A veil for the trellis," Cindy murmured, and the idea clicked into place. "I have extra fabric from these curtains in storage. The same cream silk. Would that work?"

"Yes," Nicole said, narrowing her eyes as if imagining the final result. "And we can pin it so it's removable. For photos, you can have different versions—some with more drape, some less. Dominique gets her chic, we keep our legacy."

Cindy smiled. "Let's try it."

An hour later, with open bins of fabric, a stepladder, and giant clips, they worked until the wood wore a wedding dress—soft folds cascading from the top, edges pooling slightly on the floor, the trellis's sturdy bones peeking through just enough to feel like they wanted it that way.

"Pretty," Nicole breathed, stepping aside to survey their work. "It's still *itself*, but it's styled."

The door creaked. "Whoa—what are you doing?"

Jack stood just inside, snow-scattered jacket half unzipped, a blue beanie jammed on his head at a crooked angle. He took in the white drape swathing the arch, his expression falling from curiosity to alarm.

Cindy lifted a hand in a peaceable wave. "Hey. We're just trying something."

"Why?" he asked.

"Because it beats taking it back to Grandma Irene's dormant garden," Cindy said, coming down the platform toward him. "I'm afraid the Aisle Files lady wasn't a fan."

He gave a scoffing laugh. "So?"

"So, we covered it," Cindy said.

"You can't...cover that." Jack's gaze flicked from the silk to Cindy, sharp with feeling. "It's meant to show."

Cindy moved toward him, palms out. "We're not *hiding* it. It's just...softened."

He shook his head, jaw working. "Your grandparents' initials are carved into that post."

"They still are," she said quickly. "Just...behind this fabric." She gave a small, hopeful smile. "We can pin it back for certain shots. We can even take it off entirely if you—"

Jack stepped onto the platform and placed his hand where hers had been a minute earlier, pressing the silk as if he could feel the letters through it. "I don't like this at all, Cin. We can't do this."

"Jack?" Cindy blinked at him. "Is it that important?"

"Don't you think it is?" he countered.

She threw a look at Nicole, who wore a classic "I don't want to be in the middle of this" expression.

"I'll let you guys talk," she said quickly, hopping down from the platform stage.

Cindy wanted to call her back, the business owner in her needing the support from her one-person marketing team. But the mother in her didn't want to put her precious daughter in the middle, so she just nodded and waited to talk until she and Jack were alone.

For a moment, they just looked at each other, standing long enough for Cindy to realize they were in the very same positions on that platform that they would be in on the day they remarried.

And for some reason, this felt like their first test.

"I'm not really sure what to say," she whispered. "I didn't know it was that important to you."

His dark eyes softened. "Well, it is." He swallowed and stabbed his fingers into his mostly silver hair, letting out a sigh. "We were the only couple in the whole Starling history since Irene and Owen *not* to get married under that trellis."

She nodded, remembering how and why they'd made that decision thirty years ago. They'd married at a local hotel, and the trellis was in the garden—it hadn't been a big deal at the time.

"Do you think..." She let out a laugh of disbelief. "That's why we got divorced?"

"Not why, no," he said. "But I'm superstitious about it. No one else got divorced, and everyone else married under the trellis arch. Owen and Irene, Red's sister, your Aunt Barbara and Uncle Jacob, Red and Cora, MJ and George—everyone got married under it and had really happy marriages. I believe they were...blessed."

Cindy's heart pinched at the unexpected reverence in his voice.

"That's why I really pushed for this." He glanced at the wood, making her remember his determination the day he and Cameron muscled this thing out of the old garden and into the back of the UTV.

He looked at her, voice roughened. "I need to marry you under *this*, Cin. Not a version of it. Not covered. This trellis, this arch. As it is."

Tenderness flooded her, quick and fierce. She crossed the few steps to him and rose onto her toes, cupping his cheek. "You're so sweet."

"I never want to go through..." He shook his head. "I know this is forever. I know we're not going to get divorced again. But I want our marriage to be blessed and...I believe in this thing."

He exhaled, some of the tension easing out of his shoulders. Cindy slid her arms around his waist, and he folded her in, the familiar hold she'd missed for so long settling everything inside her.

"Let me just tell Dominique right now and put this whole issue to bed." Inching back, she pulled out her phone and tapped the keys quickly, barely thinking about the composition of the note, letting raw honesty speak for itself.

The trellis was part of the Starling Room, end of story.

The response came back instantly and stole Cindy's breath.

Then we can cancel the whole thing.

"What?" Cindy blinked at the phone, then angled it to show Jack, who instantly looked as gut punched as she felt.

"For real?" he scoffed. "Then...then..." He looked from the phone to Cindy and back to the phone. After a minute, he closed his eyes. "Tell her we can move it."

"Jack! You just told me why it matters."

"It's superstitious and silly," he said, studying her. "I don't want to steal this from you. It is an amazing opportunity that's going to make your life—our lives—better. We'll just...toast under the trellis after the ceremony."

She thought about it for a long time, holding the phone, eyes welling. Who should she make happy? Dominique or Jack?

Honestly, there was no question.

"I'm not going to do that," she said.

He gave her a "get real" look and slid the phone out of her hand. "Yes, you are. I told you, we'll incorporate the trellis somehow after the ceremony. We'll get it in pictures. We'll kiss and be blessed and laugh about this. Okay?"

She just stared at him as he looked at the phone, thumbing a response.

"Okay," he answered for her.

"Jack..."

He turned and faced her, taking her hand. "I can't wait to stand here and marry you," he said.

She smiled and wrapped her arms around him, a little unsettled and uncertain...of the whole Dominique thing. With Jack, it was settled and certain.

And this battle wasn't over. When Dominique got here, Cindy would do whatever it took to persuade her to keep the trellis. She had to.

Chapter Five

Benny

As Saturday mornings went, this one was close to perfect. Sir Isaac Newton had one paw draped over Benny's Mars Rover replica like it was his personal nap mat and not the skeleton of a prized Lego project spread out on the family room floor.

The dog had a talent for locating any surface Benny needed and claiming it as his own.

Benny poked his curly brown ear with the lift arm, currently six connected Legos. "Excuse me, Professor, I need to set up the suspension system of Rover One."

The Cavapoo yawned and rolled onto his back, paws up, no shame at all. His collar tag jingled as he waited for a belly rub. Of course, Benny obliged. He couldn't say no to this dog.

He also couldn't say no to Olivia Hampton, which was why he was in a bit of a predicament, eyeing his great-grandfather, waiting for an opening to drop his little bomb.

Red sat in his recliner across the room, glasses sliding down his nose, *The New York Times* crossword attached to a clipboard that looked like it had been made the same year man went to the moon.

His coffee sat on the table beside him, cooling into that dark sludge he always swore was "just hitting its stride."

He muttered something under his breath, tapped the page, and said, "Ten letters for an

'off-hours enterprise.' Got any ideas, Benny? Like a second job you do at night."

Benny squished up his face, thinking about the words which sounded like the perfect lead to the conversation he had to have but dreaded.

"Kind of like you when you play Grumpy Santa?" he asked.

Red gave him a look over his glasses. "Not again, Benny-bean. I did my part last year. I'll get on the sleigh if I have to, but no more videos and viral fame."

Except there would be more. At least, there would be *one* more Grumpy Santa appearance.

"Oh, I know!" Red adjusted his glasses after a moment. "Side-hustle. That's an off-hours enterprise." Satisfied with that, he jotted the letters in the squares.

Benny checked the time, knowing his mom was running deliveries for the bakery this morning and would be home soon. He wanted to have this deal done before she returned, and it was going to take some convincing.

He looked down at the half-built Rover and the dog, who'd gone back to sleep, but he wasn't thinking about either one. He was thinking about the lady in charge of the Mistletoe on Main festival. And the colossal promise he'd made her yesterday.

How had that even happened?

Olivia. That's how it happened.

Grumpy Santa? Yeah, he could get his great-grandfather to play a role that came pretty naturally to him. But *ice skating?* In front of half the town?

Benny stifled a groan. What had he been thinking? He hadn't. He'd been listening to Olivia, who was a...a girl. Smart, yes. Trustworthy and solid and knew her way around a science book. But still, a *girl.*

Sir Isaac Newton rolled onto his side with a grunt. Benny leaned over and whispered, "Grandpa's gonna explode like an overcooked meatball."

Sir Isaac Newton blinked, unimpressed. Clearly, he'd already accepted Benny's fate.

Red groaned. "What's a 'Büchner pipeline' with six letters? The last one is—"

"Funnel," Benny blurted.

Red looked up so fast, his glasses almost fell off his nose. "How did you..."

"Science club," he explained. "Making crystals. We used a Büchner funnel."

"Five-letter word for genius," Red said with a grin. "Starts with a B and ends with enny-bean."

Benny smiled, pushing up as he seized the moment. Operation Grumpy, er, Skating Santa needed to launch. But how?

He brushed off his jeans and wandered into the kitchen. The tray of biscotti his mom made yesterday sat on the counter, smelling like almonds and Christmas and happiness.

Red *loved* biscotti. He said they were "tough enough to survive a dunk and sweet enough to be worth it." Benny personally thought they were like biting into one of the millions of rooftiles that came off the lodge during the renovation.

But he grabbed one, put it on a napkin, and carried it over like an offering to a grizzly bear.

"For you," he said, holding it out. "Fresh from the kitchen."

Red took it, sniffed it, and raised an eyebrow. "You want something?"

Why did the man have to be so smart about some things and clueless about technology? "Just feeling the Christmas spirit, Grandpa."

Red shot him a look that said he wasn't buying that for a second. "Out with it, boy," he said, taking a bite. "You're buttering me up like the turkey leftovers I'm going to eat for lunch. What do you need?"

Benny flopped down on the couch beside Red's recliner, pretending to study the crossword puzzle. "It's nothing major. Just...a tiny holiday opportunity."

"A holiday opportunity?" Red scoffed. "Seven letters, starts with a T."

Benny smiled. "It won't be trouble. I mean, you like Christmas, right?"

"I like sitting near a lit tree with pie and a nap in my future."

"Have you heard about the new thing they're doing in town this year? It's called Mistletoe on Main?"

Red rolled his eyes. "It's always something in Park City. Can't just shop, eat, and enjoy the snow. There has to be a tree lighting or the mayor speaking or extravagant snow globes. What is Mistletoe on Main? Sounds like there might be...kissing."

If Olivia had her way, there would be.

"There's lots of stuff, but you know the skating rink?"

He nodded, dipping biscotti into sludge and taking a big bite. "I know it."

"Well, there's going to be a performance that night. I guess real skaters doing a show or something."

Red swallowed, narrowing his eyes suspiciously. "And..."

"And they need a Santa Claus on ice and the lady who's running the whole thing asked me if I could get Grumpy Santa and I told her I would, so can you skate or at least hold onto something and go across the ice pretending like you're miserable?"

Benny took a breath at the end of the rapid-fire demand that felt like it came out as one long word.

"I won't need to pretend," he said, leaning forward on his generous belly. "I'm miserable just thinking about it."

"I know, but—"

He looked down at the crossword puzzle. "Dumbest idea I've ever heard from a smart guy."

"Red. Please listen to me."

He peered over his glasses. "Two-letter word for not a snowball's chance in hell? Oh, it's N-O. Can you spell that, Dr. Smartypants?"

He winced at the nickname because it was what

Olivia had called him for the past year. And if he was smart, he should know how to do this. What was the best angle?

Praise. Over-the-top ego stroking.

"You'd be so awesome, Grandpa!" he crooned, giving a clap to make his point. "And half the town will be there. With lots of skaters and...and people cheering. I think there would be actual thunderous applause."

Red cocked a brow and stopped Benny's ego stroking with one deadly look. Okay, new plan. Appeal to his tender old heart.

"C'mon, Grandpa. You love this town. You grew up here. You're Park City royalty and you'd be doing such a favor to that nice lady who puts on the festivals. They're desperate for a Santa and you'd be bringing a Christmas miracle!"

"Oh, Benny."

"Am I right?" he pressed, the reaction giving him hope.

"You gotta do better than that."

And the hope toppled. He blew out a breath, digging for yet another angle. "The press will be there."

Red sipped his coffee.

"It would make me happy?" Benny tried.

And dunked his roof tile.

"Good exercise?"

That got him one more cocked brow. "I'm eighty-three years old. Good exercise is a successful trip to the bathroom."

"Grandpa!" Benny tried to sound calm. "It's just...

you'd look awesome out there. You already have the beard and everything. And people *love* Grumpy Santa."

Red just looked down and picked up his pencil. "Well, what do you know? Sometimes you just see the word after staring at it for an hour." He started to scribble. "'One pulling rank is...rank odor, I bet. Like something that stinks. Sort of like all these pathetic ploys to get me to say yes."

Benny had nothing left but the nuclear option—a big, fat dose of honesty.

"Well, Grandpa, I, uh, I may have made a deal."

Red froze. "A *deal?*"

"With Mrs. Locke," Benny admitted. "She's in charge of the festival."

Red sighed and put down the pencil. "What kind of deal, Benedict?"

"The kind that involves a *win-win situation,*" Benny said quickly. "See, she wanted you as Santa for the ice show. And I wanted something, too."

He leaned forward. "What did you want?"

"Well..." Benny scratched the back of his neck. "Olivia told her that if she let Mom and Marshall Hampton work together on a gingerbread house for their block, I'd get you to do the ice show."

Red frowned. "Why would she do that?"

"Well...for the good of—"

"Do not give me a load of hooey about this town, royalty, or peace on Earth. Why did you two do that?"

Actually, it was Olivia but somehow, he was in the mix. "Because everyone wins."

"Wins what?" Red demanded. "I'll break my hip, and your mother could break..." He didn't finish but cleared his throat. "Why would you—no, why would *anyone*—think your mother wants to work with the kale-loving competition across the street?"

"Because Olivia thinks it's their...destiny."

"*Ohhh.*" He dragged out the word. "So this isn't for your mother or me or the lady in town. This is so you can gain points with a girl."

He felt his cheeks flame. "Grandpa! Come on! You know me better than that. It's for Mom! Olivia's dad is awesome. He's funny, he's smart, and he makes these protein muffins that don't even taste like cardboard. And Mom—she's awesome, too. So if they work together, they'll fall in love and get married, and then we'll all be one big happy family!"

Red's mouth hung open. "You're serious."

"It made sense at the time," he admitted. "And it was Olivia's idea, although, technically, I made the deal because I'm like your agent."

"Well, then, you're fired."

Benny sighed. "Don't you see that it could be a good idea?"

Red pinched the bridge of his nose. "Boy, you can't just arrange people's lives like chess pieces."

"I'm not arranging. I'm *nudging*. Gently." He leaned forward. "Grandpa, Mom shouldn't be alone! There's a perfectly nice former NFL player across the street and he's not married and she's not married and they each have a kid and it always works out in the dumb movies! All we're trying to do is...you know. Get me a dad and Olivia a mom."

Red stared at him, all the edges in his face softening. And, oh, no. Were those tears in his eyes? Had Benny made him cry? He hated—

"Excuse me? What did you just say, Benedict?"

Benny whipped around and stared at his mother, who stood in the doorway, arms crossed, one eyebrow raised, her cheeks pink from the cold—and, he suspected, from fury.

"Hi, Mom," he said weakly. "You're home early."

She stepped closer. "Actually, I'm right on time."

Had she heard?

Benny looked at Red for help, but the man was already folding his crossword and mumbling, "I need to go find something in the garage."

"What is it?" Benny asked, jumping on his escape. "I can find anything in that garage. What are you looking for, Grandpa?"

He threw Benny a look that was equal parts love and a warm familiar feeling that Benny couldn't name, but he certainly loved.

"My ice skates, son."

"Yes!" Benny leaped in the air, giving a fist pump of victory.

"You know, I used to be pretty good back in my day," Red said. "'Course, Eisenhower was president, but still."

As he walked out, Benny followed, but he barely made it past Mom when she snagged his sleeve.

"Not so fast, buddy."

IN THE KITCHEN, Mom sat Benny at the table and faced him directly, which was never good.

She stared him down, her eyes steady. "All right, young man. Explain."

He swallowed. "You want the short version or the long version?"

"I want the *truth* version."

He huffed out a breath and dropped all his schemes, ideas, and angles. They'd never work on Mom.

He told her the whole story about how Mrs. Locke came into the bakery, Olivia's whole *Parent Trap* thing, and the deal that they'd make one gingerbread house in exchange for Grumpy Santa on ice.

By the time he finished, her face didn't have any of the usual color under her freckles. She was pale, and her eyes looked sad and scared, and Benny wanted to go in a hole and cry for making the person he loved most in the whole world feel anything like Mom looked.

"I'm sorry," he rasped, tears springing behind his eyes. "I'll fix it."

"You might make it worse," she murmured.

"I'm sorry," he said again.

"Oh, Benny," she said. "I'm the one who's sorry."

"For what?"

"For...making you want a father."

He made a face. "I have a father, Mom."

"I heard what you said, honey. You want a dad, and Olivia wants a mom."

He shrugged. "I just got in a little deep and was trying to get Grandpa to go along with it. And he is, so... will you?"

"Will I be manipulated into working with Marshall Hampton?"

"Manipulated?"

"It means..." She smiled. "Never mind. You know what it means and how to do it. But, no, Benny, I won't."

"Why not?"

"Because it's dishonest and...calculating. I'm sad that you or Olivia thought otherwise."

"But, Mom, don't you like him? Isn't that how grownups, you know, get married?"

She laughed like he'd said something funny and sweet and sad, but wasn't it true?

"He's nice," he pressed, sensing she was starting to get it. "He even gives Sir Isaac Newton free dog treats sometimes."

"That's because he's marketing his store. Healthy dog treats, even."

"Exactly! You're both business people. You have *synergy!*"

Gracie pinched her forehead. "Honey, adult relationships aren't that simple."

"I understand complicated things, Mom. I build robots for fun."

"This is different."

"How? If you and Olivia's dad worked together on something fun, you might remember how good it feels to, you know, not be all alone."

"Sweetheart, I know you mean well. But people's hearts aren't projects you can organize."

"I know that," he said quietly. "But sometimes they just need a push."

She looked down, and for a long moment, she didn't say anything. Then she sighed and ran a hand through her hair.

"I have to tell Eleanor Locke that the arrangement is off, and I need to tell Marshall that you and Olivia cooked this up. It's not fair to anyone."

"Wait—Mom, no. Don't do that. Olivia will be mad at me."

"Then she'll be mad at you," she said firmly, checking her watch and pushing up. "But I have to tell him this was...arranged."

"What if he still wants to do the gingerbread house with you?"

"Well, then...I don't know." She picked up her purse from the counter. "I was going to have lunch with Nicole in town. I'll go a little early and stop by Craving Clean."

"Want me to come with you? I'll own up to my part in the...subterfuge."

She laughed. "Where do you learn words like that at eleven?"

"Olivia," he said honestly. "She's like a vocab queen."

Mom gave him a sad, soft look. "She's a good girl, but this was just a little too far."

He nodded, still feeling awful. "I'll go find Red in the garage and tell him not to get the skates."

The kitchen door opened and Red walked in, old brown ice skates dangling from his hand. "Just call me Dick Button."

Mom gave a dry laugh. "You're nuts, you know that? I'm running back into town. Try to stay out of trouble, you two."

She blew a kiss and passed Red to go back outside.

Red frowned, turning to watch her leave and then looking back at Benny. "She hear?"

He nodded.

"You grounded?"

"Worse. She's going to undo all my work by telling Mr. Hampton."

Red put the skates on the bench in the mudroom and headed back to the recliner like nothing at all was wrong.

"I messed up so bad," Benny said, following him.

"Oh, I don't know, Benny-bean. You tried, I guess."

Benny eyed him. "You're not mad at me?"

"Let's just say I see the merit in the idea. And I gotta hand it to you and that little girlfriend of yours—you want something, you try to make it happen."

Benny smiled weakly. "So you'll still be Santa?"

"Maybe."

Which Benny knew meant yes. "Do you think this might work?"

He shrugged. "You got them talking, so that's not a

bad thing. Now she's off to see him. Who knows? You put something in motion."

Newt came over looking for love, which he got from Benny. Red gave him part of a biscotti. And then they finished the crossword puzzle together, which made it a pretty darn perfect Saturday.

Chapter Six

Gracie

The cold caught at the back of Gracie's throat the second she stepped out of the bakery van, but the sun was high and blindingly bright. Wind buffeted the "Reserved for Sugarfall Bakery" sign on the brick wall behind her shop as she hugged her coat tighter and unlocked the back door.

It led her into the kitchen, which was bustling under the care of her store manager, Amanda Thackery. She glanced around, checking out the pie station, the cakes, and a tray of dreamy Christmas cookies just out of the oven, the familiar and comforting scents of butter, cinnamon and sweet pastry crust greeting her.

Even that comfort wasn't enough to wipe away the cocktail of emotions that had her reeling this morning.

Not one of those emotions was anger, though. She never got truly mad at Benny, even on the rare occasions when she should. The child could engineer a backyard rocket launch and light her rosemary bush on fire, and all she'd feel was pride for the flawless trajectory and gratitude that Red kept a hose handy.

Maybe she should be mad about this ruse he and

Olivia had cooked up to make a match where one would likely never be.

She stood for a moment in the kitchen, hearing the hiss of the espresso machine, the soft thud of the proofer door closing in the back. With her coat still on, she walked through her little domain, greeting the two bakers on duty, and seeing Amanda hustling at the front counter.

Was the case down? Were the cream puffs selling? Did Benny want a father that badly?

The thought was a needle running through all other thoughts, stabbing and a little painful.

Of course he did. *Of course he did.* She wasn't oblivious—she'd seen his face when his friends talked about their dads at school functions, the way he gravitated to Red like a planet around the sun. She'd made a life for him that was calm and safe and sweet, but it was a life without a father.

She'd only had her own father until she was thirty, and in those far too short years, he'd left such an imprint on her. One of the things George McBride showed her was how a man should act, and that had formed her. Benny didn't have a father or a grandfather to teach him.

Yes, he had Red—but for how long? Red was eighty-three! He'd be in his nineties when Benny was navigating the challenges of being a young man.

She slipped into her back office, delaying the trip across the street as long as possible.

What was she going to say, anyway? Gee, we can't do this because our kids *orchestrated* it?

Benny and Olivia had been stunningly...effective. She could almost admire the scheme, from a logistical standpoint. The setup was absurd, yes, but also tidy—Red would skate as Grumpy Santa, she and Marshall would collaborate on the gingerbread house.

Brilliant? Well, it was from the brains of Olivia and Benny. How could it be anything but brilliant?

But it was wrong. The meddling, the strings, the pressure. She inhaled and let the exhale firm her spine, clicking her computer to life for a distraction, hoping for a little crisis in her email that would further delay the inevitable.

There was none.

With a grunt, she pushed the chair back and walked through the bakery—which really wasn't as crowded as she'd expected it to be.

"Be right back," she called to Amanda, who waved and continued rearranging the muffin display case.

Her heart rate increased with each step across the street. She pulled open the door and instantly noticed a distinctly different aroma inside Craving Clean. It was... pure. Light. Salty fresh with no pesky...sugar.

Glancing at the tables—not full, but not lackluster—she noticed there was a line but not shockingly long. He had more customers than she did at the moment, but not a tidal wave.

As she looked around for Marshall, she wondered if maybe she should launch a "Sugarfall Light" line of products. Or increase her ads. Or run a new daily special. Or sponsor an event or—

"Can I help you?" A young man she recognized interrupted her mental panic-marketing session. "Gracie, right? I'm Roberto. Assistant manager."

"Yes, I remember. Hello, Roberto."

"Looking for Marshall?"

Well, she wasn't looking for a *Clean Puff*, that was for sure. "Is he available?"

"Actually, he ran out for a bit to get some custom cutters. Something about a gingerbread house?"

Oh, boy. She needed to talk to him and put a stop to anything he might be investing.

"Can I give him a message for you?" he asked when she didn't answer. "Or you want to text him?"

She considered saying she was pulling out of the gingerbread project without an explanation, but that would be sheer cowardice and leave the door open for more confusion.

"I'll come back later. Will he be here in an hour or two?"

"He should be," Roberto said. "I'll tell him you were here."

"Thanks." With a mix of disappointment and relief, she walked toward the door, catching one of the counter staff announce to a customer that they were out of pumpkin chia bars because they were so popular.

Should she tell the patrons that *she* had pumpkin tarts bathed in whipped cream and...

Her cell phone hummed, so she slipped it out of her bag and stepped outside, looking at the caller's name before answering.

"Hi, Nic," she greeted her cousin. "Are we still on for lunch at 501?"

"Yes, and I'm early," Nicole replied. "But be grateful because I got a table and this place is packed."

"I'll be there in a minute."

Knowing that she needed cousin time more than anything, she rushed toward 501 on Main, a favorite restaurant in the heart of the historic district.

A few minutes later, she ducked into 501's vestibule and shook out her hair, then stepped into the dining room's noise and light. Creamy tall walls, dark wood, and massive arched windows framed Main Street like a Christmas card.

The Saturday after Thanksgiving meant the tables were filled with skiers in knit caps, kids with red noses, the whole town trying to squeeze in brunch at one of Park City's best eateries.

Here, the scents were different yet again—coffee and rosemary and caramelized onions. A whole different kind of comfort on a plate.

Nicole had indeed snagged a primo table in the window and had a mug between her hands, steam curling against her face. She brightened when she saw Gracie and waved her over.

Gracie gave her a hug and shrugged out of her coat to sit down. "You look pretty, Nic."

"Oh, I have hat hair." Nicole made a face but smoothed her dark waves, which couldn't look bad before or after a hat. "You look pale. Also pretty. But pale pretty. What's wrong?"

Gracie picked up the menu like a shield. "Nothing that Park City poutine can't fix. Share some?"

"You don't have to ask."

A server arrived instantly, taking Gracie's order for the holiday hot cider, the poutine, and a promise to order something more substantial even though they knew they would split the roasted beet salad and the turkey club because they never veered from perfection.

"So," Gracie said when they were alone. "What's new? How's Cameron? Wedding plans coming along? Should I be doing anything as maid of honor?"

"After that shower you and Elise gave me last month?" Nicole beamed. "I'm still on Cloud Nine, which was the absolute perfect theme, by the way."

It had been a great event, Gracie knew, with spun sugar clouds on the champagne flutes and a heavenly theme. Elise might be wheelchair bound, but she was officially the "best woman" for her brother and had taken the role quite seriously.

"To answer your first question," Nicole said. "My fiancé is wonderful but wrapped up in paramedic finals. What's new with you?"

Gracie pressed both hands to her cheeks. "You are not going to believe what Benny did."

Nicole settled deeper into her seat like she'd just bought a ticket for a great show. "Try me."

The entire story poured out. Right at the moment where Marshall was out buying something for the gingerbread house, the poutine arrived.

Nicole had both hands over her mouth and tears in

her eyes—laughing, not crying, so hard that Gracie had to put in the rest of their order.

"They're *criminals*," Nicole said when she could finally breathe. "Absolutely ruthless. I love them."

"Do not love them," Gracie said, but she was smiling. "They've lost their minds. And that's saying a lot for those little brainiacs."

"They're clever little matchmakers," Nicole sang like it was something to celebrate.

"They're meddling," Gracie corrected. "Adorable, sure. But this is ridiculous."

Nicole's eyes were all mischief. "Is it, though? I mean, *is it?*"

Gracie felt it—that ridiculous telltale warmth climbing up her neck. "Do not."

"You have a crush on him the size of Utah," Nicole said softly, not mean, just true. "You say his name like you're trying not to smile."

"I do not say his name at all," Gracie said primly.

"Say it."

"No."

"Gracie."

She gave up the smallest smile, betraying herself. "Fine. Marshall," she said, and there it was: the warmth again. Broad shoulders. Forearms that did things to her soul.

Nicole looked purely delighted. "See?"

"Even if I *did* find him the tiniest bit attractive—"

"The tiniest bit," Nicole repeated, deadpan.

"—so what? He's across the street, and we are, at best, friendly acquaintances and bakery rivals."

"You also both *bake*," Nicole said. "Imagine what that could mean."

She took a bite of the poutine, using it as an excuse not to answer.

Nicole helped herself, then waved a fry. "Okay. Plan?"

Gracie swallowed. "I told you, the plan is to end the plan. I'm going to tell Marshall the truth. That his daughter and my son are entirely too smart for their own good. I'm going to explain what they did, we will laugh about it, and then we'll—well, *I'll*—embarrass myself and turn as red as the beets we're about to eat. Then we'll both go tell Eleanor that we're submitting two separate gingerbread houses and putting this whole ridiculousness to bed."

Nicole chewed, considering. "No."

"No?"

"No," Nicole said again, as if that settled it. "Absolutely not. Vetoed."

"You don't get a veto," Gracie said, amused.

"I do today." She abandoned the fries and leaned in, her dark eyes intense. "Gracie, listen. Those two kids are the smartest little people I know. When they come up with something, it isn't because they were bored. They know stuff. They know their parents. They know, well, pretty much everything and I, for one, think you should follow their plan."

"Please. They're eleven years old! They think love is a Lego kit."

"Sometimes, love would be easier if it was," Nicole said dryly. "Look at you. You keep everything safe. Predictable. You have your shop and your son and your lists and your pies, and it's all steady and good. You've built a *beautiful* life. But you've also built walls and... more walls."

"I don't have walls."

Nicole reached out, squeezing Gracie's wrist. "Benny showed you a door, that's all. You don't have to go through it. But don't board it up without even peeking."

Gracie stared at the window, at people passing in puffer jackets, at her own reflection ghosted back with a look on her face she recognized and didn't like. Oh, *Nicole.* She could talk a houseplant into blooming.

"Even if I... peeked," Gracie said, choosing words like stepping stones, "what if this hurts him? What if it confuses Benny? What if he thinks every friend's parent is a candidate and starts arranging weddings on the school bus?"

"Then you tell him you're the adult and you'll handle your heart," Nicole said simply. "And you will. That's the thing. You *will.* Even if nothing happens with Marshall. Even if you try this gingerbread thing and decide it's just friendship and a funny story. You can walk yourself back across Main Street and go home to your beautiful, safe life knowing you at least *tried.*"

Gracie closed her eyes.

Maybe Nicole was right. Safe had become lonely.

Predictable had become small. She had mastered the single mom juggling act so thoroughly that she'd stopped tossing anything risky into the air.

"Also," Nicole added with a wicked grin. "The man has shoulders for days. Is it a crime to enjoy building a gingerbread house next to a set of delts like that?"

Gracie bit back a laugh. "Stop."

"I won't," Nicole said cheerfully. "And what's his deal, anyway? Divorced or just separated? Why? What do we know about his life?"

"Not much," she said. "Olivia rarely talks about her mother and in the year she and Benny have known each other, I don't think she's seen the woman."

"Benny hasn't seen much of Sam."

She nodded. After some whitewater, Gracie's ex and his wife, Coco, decided to do a full court press to stay together. They had, in fact, conceived another child, due in a few months. It had kept Sam completely out of their lives.

"I don't know much about Marshall's ex—or Marshall himself, except he's a very involved father. He always comes to school events, and Olivia is a remarkable student."

"So find out about him! Use the time together to get to know who this man really is. Even if it's just as your retail neighbor, your competitor, and your son's friend's father. It doesn't have to be a Christmas romance movie. I mean, it could be, but it doesn't have to be."

Gracie wiped her mouth and stared at her food, thinking about all that. "I'm not saying yes."

"I know."

"I'm also not saying no," she heard herself admit.

Nicole's smile turned quiet and proud. "That's my cuz."

"I will think about it," Gracie said pointedly. "Think. About. It."

"Think fast," Nicole said as their salad and sandwich arrived with two plates. "Mistletoe on Main is in, what? Less than two weeks?"

Gracie plucked at a beet when Nicole divided the salad, changing the subject to Aunt Cindy's upcoming wedding, happy to listen as Nicole told her all about the pressure from the Aisle Files lady.

It was a great distraction—lots of family gossip and thoughts to share—but when lunch was over, Gracie knew she had to go back to Craving Clean with a decision.

But she still wasn't sure what it was.

GRACIE USED MORE DELAYING tactics at Sugarfall, then finally brushed her teeth, checked her makeup, and crossed Main Street with the steady chant of her intention in her head: tell him the truth, tell him the truth, tell him the—

The bell on Craving Clean's door gave its modern jingle when she stepped inside. Roberto looked up and grinned like he'd been waiting and turned to the door to the kitchen.

"She's here, boss."

She. Was he expecting her? Talking about her? She felt a flush start.

And then Marshall stepped through the door and flashed that smile that seemed to light from somewhere inside him and take Gracie's poor heart for a ride.

And the "shoulders for days" didn't help matters.

"Gracie," he said, with that jolt of pleasure that always sounded like he was happy to see her where he hadn't expected to. "Hey. I was going to come find you today. I've got something."

"I—me, too," she said, and then nearly laughed at herself. Me, too? What was she, sixteen?

He jerked his chin toward the back. "Come on. You gotta see."

She followed him through the door and into the Craving Clean kitchen, which looked much like hers—stainless steel, trays cooling, good prep lighting. It was smaller, definitely, but bustling and so clean.

There was a laptop open on a metal prep table, an image on the screen of a building that somehow looked like her shop and his, to scale, with measurements and notes about food and coloring.

Next to it were two square bakery boxes. "Okay, don't laugh," he said, sliding them toward her.

Inside one, stacks of perfectly square gingerbread panels; the other held something similar, only lighter and more textured.

"I figured we could test-drive the combo," he said, his

dark eyes hopeful. "Yours—sweet, classic g-bread, smells like Christmas. Mine—almond flour, protein powder, not as pretty, but it holds up. I thought maybe we could blend 'em—two entrances, two flavors, same structure—just like we talked about."

Gracie blinked, then laughed softly. "You baked already?"

"I did."

"You baked gingerbread with sugar and...real flour?"

He laughed, the sound somehow both boyish and deliciously masculine. "It didn't break the oven, only my healthy heart."

"Wow," she said, looking down at the two samples, wishing she could do better than "wow" but, as always, words escaped her. Along with rational thought and her purpose for this visit.

"I wanted to make sure the walls don't cave in the second a kid breathes on it. The oat version's sturdier but yours is obviously prettier. So at some point they'll have to"—he picked up one darker gingerbread and one of the pale oat pieces and fit them together like puzzle halves—"meet in the middle. Your beauty and my health."

Why, oh goodness gracious, why did that sound like a flirtatious invitation to...

To not tell him the truth.

Her chest tightened, that dangerous combination of amusement and something else. "Marshall," she said, half-scolding, half-melting.

He held up both hands, laughing. "I know, I know, I'm getting ahead of myself. I just thought if we're doing this thing, we should be prepared for it to not go perfectly smoothly, but in the end, it'll be something exquisite."

Was he talking about a gingerbread house or...them?

For a second, neither of them moved. In that flash of time, she saw something in his dark eyes—a glimmer of attraction...the faintest flicker of hope.

It was almost as if...he *liked* her. The way Olivia and Benny had imagined.

Then he cleared his throat and nudged the boxes toward her again, weirdly awkward. "Anyway. That's my play. Team effort. Sorry. You said you had something to tell me?"

Yes, she did have something to tell him. The speech she'd written in her head all the way down Main Street. The explanation that their hilarious and brilliant kids had tied them together like a pair of shoes and expected them to walk. The...

He *liked* her.

And what was she going to do about that? Slam the proverbial door in his face, stay safe in her comfort zone, and hide behind a wall that she denied she had?

Gracie swallowed. She could still say it. She had thirty ways to tell the truth, and every single one of them began with, "I need to explain what Benny and Olivia did."

He watched her with that steady patience she hadn't expected from a man whose shoulders had carried stadiums' worth of shouting. Football players understood fouls. Boundaries. Calling a play dead and starting again.

He would understand if she told him the setup was wrong.

She heard herself inhale.

"I..." She reached out and touched the edge of one of the boxes. "I wanted to tell you I have some ideas, too."

He blinked. Then an unguarded grin lit up his face. "Yeah?"

She nodded, pulse pounding in her wrists, in her throat, maybe temples and toes, too. "And I'm excited to get started."

Apparently, she was excited to stand in the same room as him, but she hoped he couldn't tell.

His laugh was warm and easy. "Okay. Okay! This is happening. For a minute there, I was bracing for a penalty flag. Got a first down instead."

She cocked her head and gave him a playful look.

"Okay. Football analogies officially over right now."

She laughed, not even caring that her cheeks felt warm. It was a bakery—minus the good stuff—so of course she was warm.

He turned the laptop toward her, shoulder almost brushing hers, the nearness of him a spark she felt and pretended not to. "I made some sketches, but let's hear your ideas first. What would you like to do?"

Nothing she could admit in this kitchen.

Pulling it together, she gestured to the laptop, rooting deep for an idea. "Um, the base is important. If we have a good foundation, we can do anything."

He smiled and angled his head. "I guess that's true about every aspect of life, Gracie."

She met his gaze and held it for enough heartbeats to make breathing a little difficult.

"I can bake a gingerbread slab on a plywood board covered in fondant so we're not moving something fragile when we set it up," she said, thanking God she could still think.

"Good, good."

"And royal icing for the outer seams," she said, her brain finally engaged, "but I want a meringue powder batch *and* an egg white batch—different dry times, different strengths in the cold. Oh, and if you insist on almond flour for part of the dough, you're going to give me the real butter."

He pressed a hand to his heart like she'd wounded him and laughed again. "Deal. And you can talk me out of monk fruit if you say the word."

She did not say *the word*—at least not the one she was thinking, which had nothing to do with baking and everything to do with what Nicole had said about doors.

They bent over the table, heads close, throwing ideas like cards. He agreed to a tiny fondant Red in a Santa suit peering in the front window, she gave in on the protein-bar "brick" trim.

There were two entrances, one a replica of Sugarfall and, on the other side, Craving Clean, and he'd promised to rig up some LED lights.

Behind them, the kitchen door swung open, and Roberto stuck his head in. "Hey, Marshall, there's a lady on the phone wants to know if 'clean' gingerbread is a thing and I said yes and then I panicked."

Marshall looked at Gracie with a conspirator's glint, both of them laughing.

"Is 'clean' gingerbread a thing?" he asked.

"It will be," she said. "Clean-ish. Don't tell her about the butter."

Laughing, he gave a nod to Roberto.

She let herself stay longer, soaking in the hum of the kitchen, the ridiculous joy of a project that wasn't safe or sensible or even particularly wise. She heard Nicole's voice one more time, not scolding now, just warm: *This might be the push you needed.*

Would she fall flat on her face? Maybe. But there was only one way to find out, so she kept the secret and set a date to bake with a man who just might have everything it would take to break down her walls.

Chapter Seven

Cindy

With her cell phone on speaker, Cindy scrolled through the online calendar, waiting for the bride to settle on a date to reschedule the venue visit— even though she already knew it wasn't going to happen.

"I think we should just cancel," the woman said, as expected. "I'm sorry, but I kind of made up my mind."

"Oh, no, no problem at all, Jenna," Cindy said brightly, her voice dipped in that professional honey she'd perfected over thirty years in hospitality. "We completely understand. Plans change. I'll go ahead and cancel the tour for January."

On the other end of the line, the young woman sounded almost apologetic. "You've been so kind, Cindy. It's just—well, I saw the Grand Hyatt's Instagram last night, and they're doing these crazy aerial shots with drone footage and custom snow machines, and it just looked so... magical. They're offering a new package, with champagne ice sculptures and a full media team, even for a wedding as small as mine. My mom said it's once in a lifetime, and...well, you know how it is."

Cindy forced a smile the woman couldn't see. Now

Grand Hyatt was after the "intimate wedding" market? Would that beast never get off her back?

"Of course I do. You need to go where you feel your day will be spectacular."

There was a soft, guilty laugh. "I really did love the look of your space, but I don't see much about it online."

"We're new."

"I guess," she said. "But I do want a place that has clout, as superficial as that sounds."

Next-level superficial, Cindy thought. "Of course," she cooed instead.

"My fiancé is a big believer in the TikTok magic."

Cindy rolled her eyes and smiled through it, promising to email the cancellation confirmation. When she finally ended the call, the cheerful lilt drained from her like air from a balloon.

She sat in her small but tidy office—the new "Snowberry Weddings HQ," as they'd dubbed the room that wasn't much bigger than a walk-in closet off the back of the Starling Room.

On a sigh, she looked at the framed photo on the small floating shelf Jack had installed above her desk. It was a perfect shot of Cindy and Jack perched on the sleigh last year, their cheeks flushed from cold air and fresh happiness.

She had to remember that no matter what happened in her new business, the rest of her life was, as Nicole liked to say, on point.

A knock on the open door pulled her back. MJ poked

her head in, a soft smile warming every feature. "Hey, you off your call?"

Cindy sighed and swiveled her chair toward her sister. "Sadly, yes. Jenna, the destination wedding bride from Sioux Falls looking for a date next fall? She just called to cancel the tour—going with the Grand Hyatt."

MJ stepped in, closing the door behind her. "Why?"

"She said she loved the Starling Room," Cindy replied, rubbing her temples, "but she saw the Grand Hyatt's Instagram account. Apparently, they have 'more clout.'"

MJ frowned. "Clout?"

Cindy gave a weary little laugh. "It's social media influence. Popularity. Basically, people want to get married at the place everyone's already posting about."

"Ah," MJ said, nodding sagely. "At the risk of sounding like our father, I'd prefer to live in a world with no hashtags."

Cindy laughed at the spot-on Red Starling imitation. "Seriously. But we don't." She leaned back, pressing her palms to her thighs. "It's not that Jenna didn't like the Starling Room—it's that we don't offer...online name recognition. And if I'm being honest, that worries me."

MJ pulled up the extra chair beside the desk and sat down, crossing her legs. "Cindy, you knew that was going to happen sometimes. The Starling Room isn't meant to compete with glitzier places. We're for the people who want something cozy and warm and intimate. Jenna just wasn't our bride."

"I know, but..." Cindy looked down. "This is my new

career, MJ. My whole second act. If I can't get people to fall in love with this place, then what was the point of all that renovation, all that planning? Snowberry Weddings has to work. It *has* to."

"It will," MJ assured her. "You've got taste, heart, and experience—and now, you've got Dominique and her Aisle Files crew on board. That's going to bring a whole new audience *and* name recognition."

"You're right." Cindy exhaled the words. "But the pressure for that to go well is through the roof. I underestimated how powerful that social media thing is. Brides don't just want pretty—they want viral."

MJ wrinkled her nose. "Viral sounds like the flu."

Cindy laughed, tension easing just a fraction. "You *do* sound more like Red every day. This is a virus we want, though."

MJ reached across the desk to pat her hand. "Dominique's coming for your wedding. The Aisle Files coverage alone will have brides from Salt Lake to Seattle calling you for tours."

Cindy looked at her sister, gratitude flickering in her chest. "You really think so?"

"I *know* so." MJ rose, brushing invisible lint from her jeans. "And you know what'll make you feel better right now?"

"What?"

"The sun and sky and mountains are perfect. Remember, we wanted to do a wedding walk-through to test the timing on the afternoon light."

"Yes." She glanced at the clock. "This is perfect, since the wedding guests arrive at four on the big day."

"And Jack arrived at three-forty-five—today."

She frowned. "Jack doesn't need to be here. This isn't the actual rehearsal. And doesn't he have a sleigh ride scheduled?"

This year, the rides were already nearly back-to-back, even without Benny's TikTok campaign. And that meant Jack was busy.

"He's between rides and he said he has some ideas."

Cindy made a face and MJ cracked up.

"I know, I know," MJ said. "Grooms and...ideas. But he so very much wants to be a part of the planning process. As I recall, the first time, he basically showed up in a tux. He wants everything to be different for you two, Cindy."

"Which is why I love him." Cindy pushed up, grabbing a notebook and ducking so her shoulder didn't bump the floating shelf as she avoided the guest chair.

Cozy, she told herself. Her new office was cozy—and tiny. The right size for a *small* business.

Picking up her phone, she followed MJ out and around the corner into the Starling Room. Inside, the space shimmered with soft, late afternoon light and suddenly that small business looked like nothing but potential.

"Oh, it's perfect," she exclaimed, imagining that this would be the time of day that guests began to arrive.

"Thank you."

She turned to look at Jack, who stood on the platform under the trellis, dressed in jeans and the white shirt he wore under his sleigh ride driver's costume. He gave her a smile as sweet as the twinkling lights behind him on the...*wait.*

What did he put on that arch?

"I'm glad you like it," he said, gesturing toward the thing she knew would cause a battle with Dominique. "I know you wanted to do something with it, so..."

He'd taken down the fabric and wrapped the wood with some artificial green garlands that looked like they were meant to spin around an outside railing and white lights that were...too white.

It was kind of awful, but he'd made an effort to dress up the trellis that he so firmly believed would somehow bring them good luck.

She wasn't about to squash that.

"I love it," she said, walking toward him. "And you."

He angled his head like the words touched him. "Same, Cinnie."

His sweet little nickname always got to her. And MJ was so right about the changes in Jack. At no point in their first marriage had Jack been this romantic, this attentive, or this much of a real partner.

For the past year, he'd been all those things, making it clear he wanted this second time around to work so much, and she loved that.

She greeted him with a warm hug. "Thanks for joining us," she whispered into a quick kiss. "I know you value your downtime between rides."

"I value this wedding more," he assured her. "So, what's the plan for today?"

"We're testing light time," she told him. "Right now, in light time, the people are arriving."

He frowned. "Light time?"

"Light is everything, Jack," MJ explained. "In fact, I'll turn the chandeliers on and grab some of the candles. Cin, you can explain the *natural* light timing to Jack."

"Of course," she said. "MJ and I have been in this room all throughout the year, all different times of day, so we tracked the changes in the light and refer to them as 'light time.' We have a system to maximize the light for every ceremony."

He laughed a little, admiration in his eyes. "Of course you do."

She laughed, too. "Can't apologize for being a perfectionist. But it's a fun concept because we've figured out that we should time weddings so the guests arrive as the sun dips close to the mountains. If we know our light time, we don't leave anything to chance."

He turned to look out the French doors and the massive windows that offered up a full mountain view. "Like right now," he said.

"Yep, and it lasts about a half-hour, though we're at the tail end of that now—sorry, I was on the phone. After everyone's seated and the wedding party is in place, if we time it right, I show up—"

"The blushing bride," he teased.

She smiled at that, loving that he thought of her like that at sixty. "I'll probably be a little flushed," she conceded. "But hopefully no one will notice because I'll arrive at that very moment when the sky and peaks are all awash with pink and lavender."

"Oh, yes," he said, nodding enthusiastically. "I know the moment you mean. It's always a big hit on the sleigh rides."

"See? You understand why we are trying to time the weddings around peak sun—which changes every month." She rolled her eyes. "So, the sky and light is a moving target."

"It's brilliant, but I can see it could stress you out."

"It shouldn't if we learn the light time throughout the year. And we definitely know winter, so our wedding should be perfect. The sky deepens during the vows, turns to twilight when we walk down the aisle together, and then the stars come out for dinner, toasts, and dancing." She grinned. "So, yes, I'm going to time the vows, the kiss, the walk, everything."

He laughed. "I better make sure the vows I'm writing fit the light time."

At the thought of him writing vows—again, something they didn't do in round one—her heart lifted. "You take all the time you need, Jack. I want to hear every word."

He reached for her, drawing her closer. "Good, because I don't care about light time. But I care about you, so I'll follow your rules."

She gave him a light kiss. "Not rules, just... guidelines."

He laughed and wrapped her into an embrace. "I just want you to be the happiest you've ever been, Cin."

On a sigh, she melted into him, forgetting light time and guidelines and everything. "I am," she promised him.

"So, what else do we do to test the light?" he asked.

Thinking about it, she turned to the trellis. "Maybe... shift the arch a few inches back to..."

"To make it disappear," Jack said on a laugh.

"No, no, I am worried about Dominique, but you know what, honey?" She gave him a squeeze. "We'll cross that bridge when the time comes. For now, let's just try to get the light right."

Jack turned her toward the windows, his arm still secure around her. "Little advice from the groom?"

"Of course."

"The sun is going to do what the sun wants to do. You can't control the clouds, the wind, the weather. Relax."

Being told to relax always had the opposite effect on her, but she tamped down her usual reaction. "I will, I promise. But the light could be the viral shot that changes everything."

"Or it could just be our wedding and not a production."

She heard the slight strain in his voice and understood, but then, he didn't realize the call she'd just completed. "I get that," she said. "But I'm stinging. I just lost a potential bride, and it was because of social media."

He winced. "Sorry to hear that."

"It's just one bride, but...somehow, our wedding got wrapped up in this marketing opportunity and I don't want to conflate the two, but I'm just trying to think through the stuff that impacts Aisle Files first, then I'll give my one hundred percent attention to our wedding."

"Because our wedding will be shown to half a million followers." He made a face. "And that's important, Cin, but I also think we'd get that business by being authentic."

He was absolutely right.

He added a kiss on her head. "So stop thinking about *light time* and start thinking *our time*," he said gently.

"I *am* thinking about it," she assured him, her tone softened. "Just...in a different way."

He squeezed her hands once more and then let go, stepping back with a nod. "I need to do a sleigh ride." He kissed her lightly. "We can go at this again later. Tomorrow? Same time, same light?"

She smiled and nodded through misty eyes, and watched him leave, knowing every nuance of Jack Kessler so well. He wasn't angry. Not exactly. But she could tell she'd missed something—something small but important.

LATER, when it was quite dark, Cindy still had the unsettled feeling when MJ came into her office again.

"Come on," MJ said. "You're done for the day."

Cindy looked up, startled. "I just—there's this email I need to—"

"Nope." MJ cut her off with a smile. "Let's have wine by the Christmas tree. Isn't that a tradition?"

"It is now," Cindy joked, happy for the moment with MJ, who marched her to the cozy living room, two wines already poured. The Christmas tree twinkled beside them, each ornament reflecting the firelight.

Cindy lifted her glass in a mock toast. "I think I blew it."

"I'm not drinking to that," MJ said. "Blew what?"

"The walkthrough. Jack tried to make it romantic and I..." She stared into the wine glass. "I started talking about camera angles."

MJ tipped her head, her eyes full of sympathy. "You're under a lot of pressure. You were just in work mode. He understands."

Cindy nodded miserably. "I just wanted it to be perfect for Aisle Files. This is our one shot to make Snowberry Weddings legitimate in the big leagues. If she loves it, we're golden. If she doesn't..."

"Then you'll try again," MJ said simply. "You always do."

Cindy looked at her sister, studying the faint lines around her eyes—the ones that came from years of joy and laughter. Tonight, they seemed shadowed by something else.

"What about you?" Cindy asked quietly. "You've been smiling at me this whole time, but it's that...half-smile. What's wrong?"

MJ hesitated, then shook her head. "Nothing. Really."

"MJ."

Her sister sighed and set her glass down. "Fine. I just —I haven't heard a word from Matt. Not an email, not a call, nothing. When he said he'd be back in a year, I guess I thought he meant Thanksgiving, which was when he showed up last time. That's come and gone."

Cindy's chest tightened, knowing that she was so wrapped up in her own personal problems that she'd nearly forgotten that MJ had issues, too.

"Have you tried contacting the attorney in town who managed the gift for us?"

When Matt had left his shocking seven-figure check, he'd done a lot of legwork ahead of time to make it easy and legal for them. He'd worked with a local lawyer who'd arranged the transfer of funds and handled opening a trust, so they weren't hit by a massive tax bill.

MJ shook her head. "That's not my place. Matt was clear in the letter that he had things he wanted to get done. To give away all he had would be like running a corporation. I'm sure he's busy, but...maybe it's just not meant to be. I mean—how would George feel?"

"If you met someone six years after he passed away?" Cindy gave a soft laugh. "George McBride would say, 'What took you so long, MJ? Time's a wastin'.'"

But MJ didn't smile at the bad imitation of her sweet late husband.

"I can see why you're concerned but I still think it's too soon to worry." Cindy leaned closer. "You really think he'd disappear forever? After everything? After giving us —you, really—a million dollars to save Snowberry Lodge and build it into something for the future? You think a man like that just walks away?"

MJ gave a sad smile. "Maybe. People change."

"Or maybe," Cindy said softly, "he's on his way back. You're the eternal optimist, remember? Don't think for one second that George wouldn't want you to be happy. And, for heaven's sake, don't give up on Matt Walker."

MJ looked at her, amusement flickering. "That's rich coming from you, Mrs. Panic About Clout and Light Time."

Cindy laughed, her heavy heart easing.

"Fair enough." She reached out, squeezing her sister's hand. "But seriously, don't lose hope, MJ. Matt's coming back, and Aisle Files is going to love Snowberry Weddings. We'll both get our happy endings."

MJ lifted her glass again, eyes glinting in the firelight. "Now that, my dear sister, I will drink to."

Chapter Eight

School was in full force the first week of December. But after the last bell mid-week, Red picked up Benny in his truck, and they headed to town for the first skating rehearsal.

The ice rink in the middle of Park City looked like a snow globe someone forgot to shake. Centered between two hotels with balconies that gave tourists a direct view of the ice, it was also the site of more than one spontaneous snowball fight, which was Benny's favorite part about the place.

The rink sparkled under strings of white lights that zigzagged across the open air, and all around, people stopped, sipping drinks, watching the event rehearsal for The Skating Spectacular with Santa.

Right now, Benny wasn't so sure "spectacular" was the word he'd use.

He pressed his mittened hands to the cold railing and squinted at the ice where his great-grandfather lumbered across the rink like a man trying to skate through peanut butter.

"Ho-ho—*whoa!*" Red bellowed, his arms pinwheeling. The red Santa coat flapped like a parachute behind him before he barely regained his balance.

The line of teen figure skaters gasped, then giggled. Their coach—a skinny lady in a sparkly tracksuit named...something—clapped twice. "Places! We take it from the top!"

Benny ducked his chin into his scarf to stifle a moan. Maybe this wasn't the best idea he'd ever had.

He loved his great-grandpa almost as much as he loved every Star Wars movie ever made, but watching Grandpa Red skate was like watching a bear do ballet. Kind of hilarious and terrifying all at the same time.

"Santa, you're supposed to *wave* to the crowd while you toss the gifts," the coach called, cupping her hands. "Remember? Big smiles! Big joy!"

"Lady," Grandpa called back, proving he couldn't remember her name either, "if I'm still upright, that's *big joy* enough!"

Plus, did she forget he was famous as *Grumpy* Santa? Wasn't that the whole idea? Benny bit his lip and tried to keep himself from jumping in to defend his best friend.

The rehearsal music started again—a happy version of "Santa Claus is Coming to Town" that sounded like elves breathing helium. The skaters zipped around, forming stars and snowflakes and candy canes while Santa stood in the center, gripping his velvet sack like it contained live dynamite.

When his cue came, he was supposed to hoist it over his shoulder, pluck small toys from it, and throw them into the crowd.

Instead, he froze.

Because that was a lot to ask of an eighty-three-year-old man.

"Mr. Starling!" the coach cried. "Now!"

Grandpa squinted, lifted one fuzzy angel doll halfway, and grumbled, "Nope."

The music screeched to a stop.

Benny moaned into his mittens. Oh, no. He knew that tone. That was *pre-eruption volcano* tone.

The coach skated over, sparkles flashing like warning lights. "What do you mean 'nope'? Red! You're Santa Claus!"

"Exactly," Grandpa said, puffing out his chest. "Santa doesn't *throw* presents at people. He sets them under the tree. That's his whole thing!"

The coach blinked. "They're lightweight toys—"

"They're *projectiles!*" Red shot back. "And this sack weighs more than a dead reindeer!"

The coach squeezed the bridge of her nose, not nearly as amused as the giggling skaters and a few of the onlookers.

"We need *movement* for the finale," she said, sounding a lot like Mom when Benny swore he'd cleaned his room but read for an hour instead. "We can't have Santa just standing there like—like—"

"Like Santa?" Red offered.

The coach's eyes narrowed dangerously.

Benny lost the fight to stay quiet. He scrambled to the gate and flipped the latch, his brain in high gear, which was saying something. "Uh, excuse me? I have an idea!"

Every head turned.

He swallowed hard but powered through, stepping out onto the ice in sneakers, moving gingerly toward Red and the coach.

"What if Santa...had a helper? Like, um, an elf who skated with him? The elf could help toss the gifts."

"I can't spare a skater to use as an elf," she said.

"I'll do it," Benny offered. "He's my great-grandpa and we actually have an elf outfit in the attic."

The coach blinked at him as though he'd suggested turning the whole show into a zombie musical. Then— miracle of miracles—her face lost some of its nasty pinch. "Go put on rental skates, kid. Let's see what you've got."

Red groaned. "Oh, for crying out loud."

Benny shot him a look. "It can't get any worse, Grandpa."

Five minutes later, Benny was wobbling across the ice in skates that were a little big. His jeans were rolled and his helmet sparkled with a red bow—the only one they had available in his size.

"Ho-ho-ho," Grandpa muttered as Benny clung to his sleeve. "This'll end well."

"Just don't fall, okay?" Benny said. "If you go down, we both go down."

"Oh, I'm aware."

The music started again. Red lumbered forward, muttering his distaste for everything about this. Benny tried to match his pace, which was like chasing a refriger-ator on wheels.

When the toy-throwing cue came again, Benny whispered, "Okay, Grandpa, you do the waving, I'll handle the pitching."

"Grumpy Santa doesn't wave," he grumbled.

"You're right, but just greet the crowd. Not with the, uh, wrong finger."

Grandpa snorted a laugh and squeezed Benny's shoulder, his watery old eyes looking down with that face that always preceded something like, "You're a keeper, Benny-bean."

But he just swallowed hard and mouthed, "Thanks."

"Don't worry, Grandpa. I got your back."

"It's not my back I'm worried about, it's my back*side*."

"You'll be fine." Benny grabbed a handful of soft toys and started tossing them gently toward the small group of spectators along the fence. The toys sailed through the air, landing perfectly in eager hands. Cheers erupted.

No-Name Coach instructed them to throw the toys back, since this was just rehearsal and she was Grinchy like that.

"Ho-ho-HO!" Red bellowed, voice suddenly booming. He even managed a small shuffle—his version of dancing.

Benny laughed and forgot the cold, forgot his wobbly knees, forgot everything but how proud he was of this ridiculous, wonderful man.

When the girls in the front row finished with a big circle around Santa and Benny, the rink exploded with applause. Red and Benny took a bow—well, Benny bowed. Red kind of bent forward to catch his breath.

The coach skated up, eyes shining. "That was fantastic! Perfect energy! Benny, you're officially part of the show!"

After the rehearsal, Benny and Red trudged up the street toward Sugarfall, where Red had parked.

Inside, his mother greeted them from behind the display case, where she was lining up mini-cinnamon rolls slathered in icing. "Hello, Santa and unofficial helper."

"You know already?" Benny asked on a sputter.

"It's Park City, honey. News travels fast." She came out with a few rolls left on a tray, leaning over to give him a kiss on the head that he didn't want but also didn't mind —not if it came with cinnamon rolls.

"Grandpa was amazing," Benny said proudly. "He only fell once."

"I *did not* fall," Red said with a scowl. "I executed a controlled descent."

"Uh-huh," Mom said, nodding for them to take a table. "Cinnamon rolls will make you both feel better. Tea for you, Grandpa? Benny, some milk?"

"Yes to everything," they said in weird and comical unison.

They sat at a corner table, quiet for a while, sharing the rolls and drinks until his mother joined them after taking care of a customer.

"Will you be done soon, Mom?"

"Yes, but I have to stay in town after we close, so you and Red can eat at the lodge."

"Do you have a cake to bake or something?" he asked, taking a sip of milk.

"Actually…" She gave him a funny look. "Eleanor Locke has called a quick Mistletoe on Main planning meeting." She cleared her throat. "Marshall and I are going to meet there to get approval on our gingerbread house idea."

Benny sat up a little straighter. "Wait. What? You're doing that…with him?"

Her cheeks got a little pinker. Well, Mom was basically an Olympic-level blusher, and it told Benny a *lot*.

"I'm not happy that you interfered, but I'm not quitting." She wiped her hands on her apron. "It's good marketing. And the combo structure is really cute and might actually win the award for best gingerbread house."

"There's an award?" Benny blinked.

"A plaque, not money, but we both agree it will be good attention for our shops." She gave him a warning look. "It's *business*, Benny. And I still am telling you to please stay out of adult affairs."

He sighed, slumping. "Yes, ma'am."

"I mean it."

"I know." He fiddled with his milk glass. "I am sorry, Mom."

She angled her head with a kind of sad look in her eyes. "I'm sorry you want a father so much you pulled a stunt like that."

"'Specially when you have a great-grandfather," Red said. "I mean, the words *great* and *grand* are in my title. What else do you need?"

Benny smiled. "Nothin', Grandpa."

"Oh, look, there's Olivia walking her dog," Mom said, gesturing toward the window. "Might be a good time to deliver the same 'do not meddle' message to her."

Benny nodded, finished his cinnamon roll, and downed the milk. "I'll be back in a minute, Grandpa."

"Take your time, Benny-bean. I need my rest from all those triple axels."

SNOW CRUNCHED under Benny's boots as he crossed the street toward the girl in the bright purple parka being dragged by a blur of fur.

Kat, Olivia's border collie, spotted him and bounded forward, nearly yanking Olivia off her feet.

"Benny!" Olivia cried, laughing. "Hey! You survived skating with Santa! I heard you're in the show!"

"Yeah." He shoved his hands in his pockets. "Listen, we gotta talk."

Olivia's eyes widened. "What happened? Is Red okay? Didn't fall, did he?"

"No! Well, once." He sighed. "It's about...our plan."

Her expression brightened. "Oh! The Operation Gingerbread Romance Initiative?"

"I thought it was...Mistletoe Madness or something."

"Whatever. My dad's so excited! He showed me the sketches and told me they are going to the meeting together tonight." She held up her leash-free hand for a high-five. "WTG, soon-to-be stepbrother."

He groaned. "Olivia, you have to stop."

"What? Why? Don't you want them to fall in love and get married?"

"Not as much as you do," he said, kicking at a patch of snow. "Anyway, it's not about...all that stuff. They're doing it for marketing reasons, so no more dumb... romance." The word tasted like dirt in his mouth.

Olivia frowned. "That doesn't make sense. My dad's excited. He was humming while chopping carrots last night. *Humming,* Benny. He likes her. I can tell."

"That's not proof."

"It's *data,*" she insisted.

"Olivia," he said patiently, "we can't interfere anymore."

"But—"

"My mom told me to stay out of adult stuff. So we're staying out. End of story."

Kat barked as if she agreed, but Olivia planted her boots and lifted her chin. "No. We're not giving up."

"Olivia!"

"Come on, Benny. They're already working together. They have chemistry. They're single—"

"Stop saying that word!"

"—and they like Christmas!"

"Everyone likes Christmas."

"Exactly! Common interests!" Her eyes gleamed with determination. "We just have to...increase the probability of romance."

He groaned. "You can't make people fall in love. It's not like science."

"Says who? There's chemical attraction, emotional resonance, shared responses—"

"They're not your personal lab experiment, Olivia."

She just grinned, which made him so mad, he could scream.

"If I can *prove* they like each other, will you help me, Benny?"

Benny could probably already prove it with one picture of his mother blushing every time Marshall's name came up. "How?" he asked.

"The usual—observation, testing, controlled conditions. Maybe a little..." She fluttered her fingers like the Wicked Witch about to throw apples. "*Assistance.*"

"Olivia."

"Come on," she said, laughing like this was a game. "We're the smartest kids in sixth grade. We can solve this."

"There's nothing to solve," he said. "Just leave them alone and maybe..."

"Maybe nature will take its course?"

He wasn't at all sure what she meant by that, but he wouldn't admit that.

"And if you won't help, fine." She shrugged and flicked her fingers. "I'll do it myself."

"Do what?" Although he wasn't sure he really wanted to know.

"I don't know yet," she said. "But I'm going to do some research. I'm going to put together all the elements necessary for the human brain to think it's in love. Then

I'm going to make it happen. Yes, I am. If you don't help, I don't care."

He stared at her, thinking about the hurricane category scale they'd learned in science this afternoon. Olivia Hampton was a Cat 5. A human tornado. An avalanche. Name a disaster, and she was it.

Kat barked again, then promptly dove into a snowbank, emerging covered in white. Olivia brushed her fur. "See? Even Kat believes."

"Kat's trying to hide from your insane ideas."

She let out a laugh that sounded like the bells around Copper's neck when he was pulling the sleigh.

"Do you want to be kept apprised of my plans or are you one hundred percent out?" she asked.

Apprised? Who said apprised? Besides Benny, no one. Except...Hurricane Olivia. "Keep me *apprised*," he muttered, turning away. "I better get back to the bakery."

A minute later, he slumped into a seat across from Grandpa.

"How'd the debrief with your partner in crime go?"

Benny shook his head. "She's still scheming. No matter what I said, she was, like...determined."

"Women. Can't live with 'em, can't bear life without 'em."

Oh, Benny could bear it all right.

Grandpa leaned back, eyes twinkling under bushy brows. "So, what's the latest plot?"

"She wants to *prove* my mom and her dad are secretly in..." He couldn't say the word love. "Into each other," he finished. "Or do some kind of wacky experiment that will help them get there. What am I going to do?"

"When you're in a swamp called 'lady logic'? There's no easy way out."

Benny huffed out a breath. "But she wants to do this and I should help, just to make sure she doesn't do something that really upsets Mom, but if I help, *that* will upset Mom." He grunted, hating circular logic.

Grandpa leaned forward, with that same look he'd given Benny on the ice. "You got a good heart, Benny-bean. That's why you keep getting yourself into trouble. You want everyone to be happy."

"Is trying to make everyone happy bad?" he asked.

"Nah. It's what makes you a Starling man." He reached across the table and tousled Benny's hair. "Which we've been missing for a few generations. All those girls!" He rolled his eyes. "You just learn to pick your battles. Like, say, don't pick one with your mama."

His *mama.* The one who would kill him, ground him, remove all computer privileges, and probably take away any hope of getting that phone if he did exactly what Olivia was thinking about doing.

Benny looked out the window, just in time to see Olivia walk inside Craving Clean with her dog, making his whole chest feel...weird.

Was that because maybe Olivia was right? Or because he just couldn't say no to that girl?

Chapter Nine

"...And remember," Eleanor Locke announced, clutching her clipboard to her chest, "the day and night is called 'Mistletoe on Main' for a reason. We want bushels of mistletoe for this one. We will expect no less than a hundred kisses, three proposals, and at least one spontaneous wedding!"

Nervous laughter rippled through the crowded Park City Community Hall. Sitting inches from Marshall, Gracie waited for the warm rush of blood to her cheeks at the thought of...kissing.

But there was none, thank goodness.

Next to her, Marshall leaned a centimeter closer, making her aware of nothing but his masculine scent and the light pressure from his shoulder.

"We should do little mistletoes hanging over both entrances," he said, clearly thinking about the design they'd just had approved and not...kissing.

The Mistletoe on Main committee had loved their joint concept and Eleanor made such a huge deal over how adorable it was and how it promoted peace on Earth —or at least peace between rivals.

Whatever, they were committed to this now.

Eleanor droned on about the event, chatting about live reindeer and the tree lights, the carolers and an elf parade, and, of course, The Skating Spectacular with Santa.

A few people in the front row argued about the placement of the Nativity scene, and old Mr. Knowles stood up and asked that his golden retriever be allowed to play a sheep.

Marshall inched closer again. "And here I thought I was moving to a sophisticated ski resort town."

"Emphasis on *town*," she said, smiling up at him. "Small, sweet, and not sophisticated."

"I love it," he murmured, his dark eyes glinting. "I feel like I'm in *Gilmore Girls*."

She wasn't sure what surprised her most—the fact that he watched girly TV shows or liked the small-town vibe. But what really surprised Gracie was the fact that, despite the proximity to a man who turned her legs to Jell-O, she was surprisingly comfortable.

From the moment they'd started to walk together to the meeting, Marshall had put her at ease. She'd let him lead their two-minute presentation of their gingerbread house, but he had given her praise and credit and had talked to every person with an amazing amount of humility.

Every time someone mentioned his NFL career, he acknowledged the compliment and interest and asked a question about their lives and jobs.

Pure class, as MJ would say, and it went a long way to making Gracie feel completely relaxed with him.

When Eleanor adjourned the meeting and the room filled with chatter, laughter, and the crinkle of puffy jackets as everyone rose, Gracie decided she couldn't remember the last time she'd enjoyed a town meeting so much.

They both talked to a few more people, then made their way outside to find Park City glittering in holiday finery.

The Christmas lights strung from lamppost to lamppost twinkled red, gold, and white, and the air smelled like cinnamon and firewood. The street looked like a postcard for small-town holidays and Gracie was oddly proud of her home as she tugged her scarf tighter.

"That went better than expected," she said as she and Marshall fell into step together, heading down the sidewalk.

They passed the twinkling storefronts and spotted the window of Sugarfall, shining soft and warm a block away. Across the street, Atticus Coffee's windows glowed with amber light, wreaths on every pane.

"Look," he said. "Atticus stays open late for the whole month of December."

She nodded, then glanced up at him. "You think you want to extend holiday hours?"

He laughed. "Not everything is about work, Gracie. I think I want to extend our evening together." He gestured toward the beloved coffee and tea shop, which looked achingly inviting in the snow. "I've got the babysitter for another hour, so...tea?"

Her heart did a strange little skip when she nodded.

Not the usual skip of overanalyzing or feeling the tension that came with life as an introvert, either.

The fact was, she couldn't dream of saying no.

"I'd love that," she said. "But only if you promise not to judge me for putting sugar in my lavender Earl Grey."

He made a face and grunted, hammering his chest with his fist. "You're killing me, Ms. McBride."

She laughed as they crossed the street and walked up freshly salted steps to the charming brick building. Then they stepped into a warm Park City landmark that was part coffee shop, part bookstore, and one big community.

The café was all cozy Christmas, with strings of fairy lights looped across exposed beams. A tiny tree sparkled in the corner, and someone had stacked gingerbread-scented candles by the counter.

Atticus was hopping, proving that extended hours made a lot of sense at this time of year.

They snagged a table near the bookshelves and Marshall went to the counter and got their order, smiling kindly at the barista.

At the table, Gracie pulled off her gloves and slipped out of her jacket, eyeing the snowflakes drifting past the streetlights outside the window.

Marshall came back with drinks and took the seat across from her, leaning the backpack he'd brought to the meeting against his chair.

The warmth seeped into Gracie's fingers as she wrapped her hands around her cup.

"I guess this place is also our competition," he mused, sipping his tea.

"In a way, but Atticus has a vibe all its own," she told him. "It's the embodiment of Park City, which is still a little bit historic mining town and a little bit upscale ski haven. Also, this time of year? Brace yourself. We go all-in."

He looked around, his expression thoughtful. "It's funny. I didn't think I'd like that kind of thing—small-town festivals, neighbors who know your middle name. But I do. It's... charming. And it's been so good for Olivia. She loves it here, you know."

Gracie smiled. "She's a great kid. All I've ever wanted for Benny was a good friend and she absolutely fits the bill."

He nodded, swirling his tea absently. "He's a perfect, sensible foil for her tendency toward wild fantasies."

Like Marshall and Gracie falling in love and getting married.

She just smiled and they sat quiet for a moment, the soft hum of conversation around them. Taking a sip, Gracie found herself studying his face—the strong line of his jaw, the dimple that appeared when he smiled, the gentleness in his eyes. Right then, she just wanted to know more about him.

"I know you played for Pittsburgh, but is that where you grew up?" she asked.

He shook his head. "Across the state in Philadelphia, actually. Born and raised in the city. My mom worked two very demanding, physical jobs—hospital aid and waitress. I spent a lot of time on my own. Not a lot of chill places to hang out, so I found the football field."

"Once again, sports saves the day."

"Did it ever," he said. "Football gave me focus. Something to chase that didn't involve getting into trouble."

Gracie leaned forward slightly, elbows on the table. "You must have worked really hard to play professionally. I can't imagine the dedication that takes."

He shrugged, but there was pride in his eyes. "I figured out by tenth grade that if I hustled hard enough, I could get a scholarship. Penn State came calling when I was seventeen. Best day of my life."

She smiled. "Until the Steelers, right?"

His laugh was quiet, almost self-deprecating. "Yeah, that was surreal. My mom cried for a week straight. I thought I'd made it. Then I learned fame's a funny thing —it gives you everything except the stuff you really need."

Gracie tilted her head. "Like what?"

He looked at her, serious. "Peace. Stability. Trust."

Something in his tone made her chest tighten. "You have that now, though," she said. "At least I hope you do."

He gave her a small, grateful smile. "I do. Thanks to Olivia. And this town."

"What brought you here?" she asked. "Why Park City?"

"I knew people who had second homes here and I'd visited," he said. "I like the winter vibe, although after having spent a year here, and experiencing the other seasons? I like the year-round vibe, to be honest. Hiking, biking, skiing, and I have what looks like a great business. Long way to go," he added quickly. "But I'll get there."

She considered asking about the business, but she didn't want to get back into their competition for customers. This was too easy and fun with no "work" in the mix.

"You definitely have a local feel, Gracie," he said. "Born and raised in these mountains, I presume?"

She nodded. "I've never lived anywhere but here. My family's owned Snowberry Lodge for three generations. Park City was my home long before the Sundance Film Festival brought all you celebrity types here."

"It's still a great small town." He glanced around again. "I like the predictability of the place. That sense of, I don't know, everything you need is right here. I like festivals and events." He lifted his brows. "If Eleanor finds out, I'll be on the next committee because I won't be able to say no."

She smiled, caught off guard by how sincere he sounded. "So, you're a softie, huh?"

"Don't tell anyone," he said. "Ruins my tough-guy image."

They both laughed and sipped their drinks until Marshall leaned back in his chair. "Would it be super out of line for me to ask about Benny's dad? I mean, since we're trading origin stories."

Gracie hesitated, tracing a finger along her mug's rim. She wasn't used to talking about Sam, not like this. But something about Marshall—his open, steady gaze, the way he wasn't prying, just *listening*—made it feel just fine.

"Sam and I met when I was studying to be a pastry

chef at a local cooking school," she said slowly. "He'd moved to Park City looking for the next boomtown. He worked at the local restaurant where I interned on the pastry line. And we...got serious pretty fast."

Marshall didn't interrupt, just nodded slightly.

"When I told him we were going to have a baby, he panicked. I wanted to get married but he said he wanted to go to Vegas." She gave a soft laugh. "I really thought he was going to scope out chapels and such for a quickie wedding. But he got a job in a casino and...never came back."

"Ooh." He angled his head in sympathy. "That's rough."

"He said he'd come back, then said he'd visit. He does, once in a while. He calls on most birthdays and at Christmas. He sends the occasional check, but he's married with a child and one on the way." She looked down, hating that she'd fallen for someone who just didn't love her enough to stick around and be a man, a father, and a husband. "I used to be angry about it, but now I'm just... grateful I got Benny out of the deal. He's my whole world."

"With good reason," he said, a look of admiration in his eyes. "You've raised him alone?"

She shrugged. "Technically, yes. But you met my family at the dog event last Christmas. My mom and aunt, my grandfather and cousin—we're a pack. Benny's been well-loved and I've been emotionally supported. We live in a big house on the Snowberry property where I grew up, like my mother and grandfather."

"Very historic and grounding," he said. "And great for Benny. I think family is so important. My mom died three years ago and..." His voice grew taut. "That's why I left Pennsylvania. I'd moved her to Pittsburgh, and she lived with Olivia and me. With her gone, I had to start over."

She searched his face, the obvious and unspoken question hanging between them. "I thought I heard Olivia say something about joint custody once? Her mother is..."

"Her mother is...Bianca." He said the name as if it stung a little. "We met when I was with the Steelers. She was...wild. Gorgeous. The kind of person who makes every room tilt sideways when she walks in. I was mid-career, riding high on success, and honestly, too dumb to see what she was really after."

Gracie stayed quiet, letting him continue.

"She got pregnant about three months after we met," he said. "I was scared out of my mind, but I was also thrilled. I always wanted to be a dad. I thought maybe that would make everything make sense." He gave a humorless laugh. "So I did what seemed right. I married her."

"You were trying to do the honorable thing," Gracie said, part of her wishing Sam had that much respect, but part of her grateful he didn't.

"Yeah," he said. "And for a while, I thought it might work. But when Olivia turned four, and I retired from the NFL, well, I guess the thrill was gone. Bianca started disappearing—nights out that turned into weekends, and long absences with 'friends' I'd never met. When I caught her cheating, it was almost a relief. At least then I knew."

Gracie's breath caught. "Marshall..."

"She filed for divorce, took a hefty settlement, and made it clear she wasn't interested in the whole co-parenting thing. We have joint custody on paper, but she makes just about zero effort to see Olivia. Kind of like your ex."

She looked skyward. "Some people shouldn't be parents, but I have to say—Olivia is a gem."

"So's Benny," he said. "But thank you. Credit to my mother, honestly, who did double duty as grandmother. It's harder now, without her, but Olivia is...everything."

For a long moment, Gracie fought the urge to reach across the table, to take his hand, to tell him how impressed she was. But she wasn't *that* comfortable. Instead, she just smiled.

"She's lucky to have a dad who loves her so much."

"I'm lucky to have her," he said. "She runs rings around me intellectually, though."

"Welcome to my world," Gracie joked.

"To single parents of Mensa candidates." He lifted his mug for a toast. "A special challenge."

She met his mug with hers just as their gazes locked. For a long moment, the tea shop seemed to quiet, the lights and people and scent of herbal teas all disappeared as her entire focus sharpened on this man.

"I guess we have a lot in common," she said, surprised at how tight her voice was. "Being a single parent is very hard, no matter what kind of family or village you have."

"Olivia seems to think so," he said. "She's always encouraging me to contact you, but..."

Gracie waited, her brows rising. "But..."

"Well, I still feel like I blew into town and put a damper on your business."

"You kind of did," she joked, "but we'll survive."

"It's not exactly great for mine to be across the street from the world's most desirable cream puffs."

She laughed and shifted in her seat, knowing that the conversation had led to the fact that their kids had played matchmakers. She should tell him that right now.

He studied her face, looking into her eyes long enough to elicit a blush, but she told herself that anyone would have warmed under that kind of scrutiny.

"The thing is," he said slowly, making her wonder where he was going next. "I haven't...I don't..." He swallowed. "I have a hard time trusting people," he finally said. "Maybe now that you know my history, you understand."

"I understand," she said.

If he wasn't a trusting man, should she tell him about what the kids had done...or not?

Would he be mad? Disappointed? Amused? Would he wonder why she hadn't told him when they first talked about it?

"I should probably get back," he said, tucking a folded napkin next to his mug as if he somehow thought his confession was...too much. "Olivia's sitter will think I disappeared."

"Yes," she agreed. "Benny's great-grandfather tends

to conk out by eight and if that child is left to his own devices, our Christmas tree will run on robotics by the time I get back."

They stood, pulling on coats and scarves. As they stepped outside, the cold air wrapped around them, crisp and biting. Snow fell thicker now, swirling in the glow of the streetlamps.

They walked in silence for a block. Gracie could feel the warmth of him beside her, that same quiet comfort all over her.

"This was fun," she said, smiling up at him.

"You sound surprised." He laughed. "I didn't even make you eat carrots and chia seeds."

"I am surprised," she admitted. "I'm glad we got to know each other."

They slowed when they reached Sugarfall, which was locked up tight for the night. He turned to her, looking down.

"So am I," he said. "And next time I see you, we will create the best gingerbread structure this town has ever seen."

She laughed and pulled out her keys. "I'm going to walk through to my car in the back. Good night, Marshall."

"You okay to go alone?"

She smiled, touched by the protectiveness she so rarely got to experience. "I am, thank you."

"'Night, Gracie."

"Good night, Marshall."

Inside Sugarfall, the lights were still on in the display

case, casting a golden glow. Back in the quiet, warm kitchen, Gracie leaned against the counter and closed her eyes.

He hadn't made her a nervous wreck. She hadn't been shy, scared, or stuttering like a crushed-out fool.

Did that mean she didn't really like him?

Or that she really, really did?

Chapter Ten
Cindy

Cindy paused in the doorway of what used to be her office, taking in the subtle changes since it had become *Jack's* workspace. The soft plaid curtains she'd hung back when it was her domain were still there, but the desk had migrated closer to the window, and a few framed skiing photos—actual Olympic shots—had replaced her collection of color-coded calendars.

A signed poster from the '02 Salt Lake Games hung behind his chair, the athletes frozen midair against that familiar bright-white snow. It felt...different, but in a good way. Like him.

"You look busy," she said, leaning on the doorframe.

Jack didn't look up right away. He was focused, tapping something into his computer, glasses perched on his nose. Somehow, Jack had become a sixty-something man, but she could still see that young skier she'd fallen hard for thirty years ago.

Finally, he hit a key, leaned back, and smiled. "I was. Then my favorite distraction showed up."

Cindy rolled her eyes, but she was smiling. "Smooth."

He stretched, arms overhead, his bones letting out a

soft creak that probably started back in those Olympic days. "You caught me at the perfect time. Just finished the morning reports from the sleigh rides."

"More today?"

"I'm actually free until four o'clock. Want to play hooky?" He made a face. "Do they still call it that?"

"The over-sixty set does," she joked, sliding into the chair across from him. "Tell me about this hooky idea of yours."

Jack closed his laptop and gave her his full attention. "You. Me. Town. Lunch. Oh, and I have a special errand to run and...yeah. I was going to surprise you, but you can come with me."

"Surprise?" Her brows lifted. "I like the sound of that. Gracie was going to drop off a wedding tasting order, Nicole was trying to fix the twinkle lights in the Starling Room, and MJ..." She angled her head and sighed. "Honey, I'm worried about MJ."

"Why?" He leaned forward, concern in his dark eyes.

"She's been quiet and down, so unlike her. She hasn't heard a word from Matt since he left."

Jack rubbed the back of his neck, thinking. "He said a year in that famous letter that should probably have been a secret but we all read."

Cindy smiled. "She might have framed it and hung it in her new apartment up on the third floor." And that smile faded. "Which is why I'm concerned about her. Technically, that year is up on New Year's Eve, but..." She hesitated, glancing at the snow-dusted pines outside the window. "I honestly thought he'd be back by now. I even considered sending him an invitation to our wedding."

He raised a brow. "Would that have been wrong?"

"I don't know." She twisted her engagement ring absently. "MJ's so hopeful, but what if he's not coming back? I don't want her heart broken all over again."

Jack's expression softened. "Maybe he's just...taking longer than planned."

"Maybe." Cindy frowned. "I was thinking about calling that lawyer who handled everything—the trust, the checks, all that paperwork. You remember him?"

"Richard Lowe."

"Yes. Maybe he's heard something. Maybe Matt's been in touch with him. Would that be out of line for me to do?"

"No." Jack pressed his hands on the old mahogany desk. "I have an idea and, sorry, but it's actually genius."

She chuckled at that. "Talk to me, genius."

"Let's drive into town and see Richard face to face, maybe get a real sense of what he knows about Matt's whereabouts. Then we run my secret errand and grab lunch at Kaneo."

"You had me at secret errand, but then Kaneo? Yes, please."

She'd barely finished and he was up and around the desk, eager to go. "I love a day off with my girl."

As he pulled her up from the seat, she laughed and leaned into his hug. "And I love being your girl."

Not an hour later, they were strolling down Main Street, bathed in bright Utah mountain sunshine. The air carried a crisp brightness that brought Park City alive, dressed in red bows tied to lampposts, evergreen garlands winding up porch railings, and storefront windows painted with swirling snowflakes.

Cindy loved this part of town—the historic mining-era buildings stacked along the hills, the mix of old and new everywhere.

Holding hands, they paused outside a modest brick building with a brass plaque that read *Lowe & Jacobs, Attorneys at Law*. She and MJ had come here a few times early in the year, still dumbstruck from the gift they'd received from plumber-turned-millionaire lottery winner Graham Matthew Walker.

Richard Lowe had patiently walked them through accessing the funds that Matt had carefully protected for them. With that job in the past, would he know anything about his mysterious client's whereabouts or plans?

She sure hoped so.

Inside, a young receptionist with bright red lipstick looked up and smiled. "Hi, there! Can I help you?"

Jack stepped forward. "We're here to see Richard Lowe but we don't have an appointment. This is—"

"Cindy Kessler," the woman finished.

"Oh, you remember me?"

"And your sister, MJ," she said, adding a wink and leaning in to whisper, "We don't get cases like yours very often."

Cindy imagined that was true.

"Let me get Rich," the woman said, slipping out from behind her desk.

They waited on a leather sofa until a door opened, and Richard Lowe appeared—a man in his late fifties with kind eyes, a trim beard, and the exact same conservative tie he'd worn the day she met him.

"Hello, Cindy," he said warmly, shaking her hand first, then turning to Jack. "And we have met. Jack Kessler, right?"

He returned Richard's warm handshake. "Yes, sir. Hope we're not barging into your billable hours."

The other man laughed and waved them into the offices. "It's fine and always good to see you. Would either of you like coffee or water?"

"No, we're good," Cindy said, following him down a wide hallway that smelled faintly of lemon and hummed with busy people behind open doors. "We really just wanted five minutes of your time today."

"Whatever you need." He led them into his office, which was comfortably cluttered with paperwork and books, with a window that looked out at Main Street like a postcard view.

"So," Richard said, gesturing for them to sit on two chairs in front of his desk while he took the large leather seat behind it. "How's the renovation at Snowberry? Have you finished the Starling Room?"

"We have," Cindy said. "And it's beautiful."

"We're getting married there in less than two weeks." Jack took her hand. "We're going to have the inaugural event in that room."

"Wow, congratulations! But..." He lifted a brow. "I

guess I thought you were already married. Same name and all."

"We were," Cindy said.

"It's our second time around," Jack added, making the other man break into a huge smile. Cindy had long ago noticed that, universally, people loved a second-chance romance.

"Well, that's terrific. So happy for you."

They thanked him and, still holding Jack's hand, Cindy leaned forward. "We'd actually love to invite Matt Walker, so...we were wondering if you'd heard from him lately."

He folded his hands, a frown folding. "I'm afraid I haven't heard from him since last...spring, was it? April or May. I can look up the client log." He turned to his computer and tapped some keys to bring the monitor to life. "The trust paperwork was finalized, the funds dispersed, but I did check in with him...yes, it was May tenth and he was in..." He drew back. "My notes say he wanted to touch back to be certain that all the funds he'd given you were managed properly and the trust assured that you paid no taxes on the gift."

So he was still thinking about MJ and Snowberry Lodge—that was encouraging. "Does he still have the same mailing address?" Cindy asked.

"A post office box, yes. And an email, though I can't promise he checks it often. Would you like me to give it to you?"

"Yes, please."

He scribbled the information on a notepad and tore

off the page, sliding it across the desk. As she took the paper, she sighed heavily enough for Richard to give a sympathetic smile.

"I certainly sensed Matt was a man of his word," the attorney said. "And if something happened to him, I would likely get some kind of notification."

"So we shouldn't worry, right?" Jack asked, squeezing her hand. "He did say he'd be back in a year."

"I really can't speak for him. I put him in touch with an accounting firm in Florida because he wanted to start the process of turning his winnings into a foundation to help others." He gave another smile. "I don't imagine someone who wants to share that much money with other people is a person you'd need to doubt."

"I agree," Cindy said, folding the paper and sliding it into her purse. "Thank you, Richard."

"I wish I had more to offer," he said. "But if I do hear something, I'll reach out right away."

"Thank you," she said again, standing. "And Merry Christmas, Richard."

"And to you both," he said warmly. "Give my best to MJ."

They said goodbye and headed back to the street, both quiet as they digested the lack of new information.

Outside, the light hit just right—sharp and golden against the mountain backdrop. Cindy tucked her hands in her coat pockets and looked down Main Street, where a group of carolers were warming up in the park and a few kids were running around in the snow.

It was festive and fun, but her heart was heavy. As if

he sensed that, Jack put his arm around her shoulders and pulled her close. "We tried."

"I just hate the thought of MJ waiting for something that might not come."

"She's tougher than she looks," he said gently. "But I know what you mean."

They walked a few steps in silence, passing the art galleries and boutiques decked in fairy lights.

Finally, Cindy exhaled, shaking off the heaviness. "All right, Mr. Secret Errand Man. What's next?"

Jack's grin returned. "This is the fun part!"

"Everything is with you."

He laughed, liking that. "This one is special, though. Come on."

As she slipped her hand through his and they continued down the street, the tension that had been coiling quietly inside Cindy for weeks seemed to ease. For the first time in a long time, she felt exactly what she'd been craving—peace, contentment, and full-body relaxation.

"I needed this," she said on a sigh.

"You need to work less," he replied.

She slid him a look. "Is this history repeating itself, only with role reversal?" She asked the question lightly, but it wasn't light, not by any means.

Jack's obsession with skiing, then his job at ESPN, was acknowledged by both of them to be the crack that broke their foundation and led to their divorce eleven years ago.

"We can't let history repeat itself," he said softly.

"We won't."

His eyes flashed slightly, and she braced for a comment about her laser focus on building Snowberry Weddings, but he just turned a corner and guided her down a side street where the buildings crouched closer and the sidewalks didn't get quite the snow cleanup that Main Street did.

Cindy recognized a few independent shops that had survived the years—the cobbler who still could fix anything with laces, the record store enjoying a resurgence of vinyl popularity.

Jack slowed in front of a storefront trimmed with tin cut-outs of snowflakes and a carved wooden sign that had been there as long as she could remember: Hearth & Hollow. The name was painted in cream, the ampersand fat and cheerful.

Cindy let out a laugh of delighted surprise. "No way, Jack Kessler. I haven't walked into this store in...decades."

"But we used to love it, remember? We always came here to get special keepsakes for Nicole when she was a little girl."

"I remember," Cindy said gleefully, letting him open the door for her.

A bell chimed with a warm note of welcome. Inside, the little shop smelled like cedar shavings and orange peel. Shelves climbed from the floor to the pressed-tin ceiling, crowded with handmade toys, carved ornaments, old-world puzzles, and an artful clutter of snow globes—tiny cities, tiny deer, tiny skiers mid-swoop.

In the back, behind the register, an ancient lathe

rested like a retired workhorse, and beside it, a glass cabinet glowed with snow globes that were custom-made to commemorate special occasions or replicate beautiful homes.

"Hello there, Jack Kessler!" sang a voice from somewhere between the nutcrackers and the papier-mâché stars. A woman popped out—a small, spry creature with a silver braid as thick as a rope and spectacles perched halfway down her nose. "Yes, before you ask, it's ready. This must be Cindy. I'm Marta."

"Hello, Marta," Cindy said, shaking the hand the woman offered. Jack had been coming in here without her?

They chatted about weather and tourists and skiing, then Marta held up a finger to ask them to wait. "Should I wrap it, Jack?"

"Yes, please," he said, a glint in his eyes that Cindy simply couldn't read.

The woman disappeared into the back and Cindy eyed her once and future husband. "What are you up to, Jack?"

"You'll see. Let's look around. Maybe we'll find something for Nic again."

They scanned the shelves and racks, holding hands like they had when they were young parents, eyeing wooden puzzle boxes, handmade puppets, and a cuckoo clock so elaborate it took her breath away.

Marta reappeared, her arms cradling a box wrapped in pearl-white paper with a red-and-white baker's twine tied in a bow. A tiny wooden snowflake dangled from the knot. She set the box on the counter with a satisfied pat.

"This one is exquisite," she whispered. "Fritz put love into it."

Jack just gave her a smile. "You have my card on file."

"Then you're all set, Jack." She dropped the wrapped box into a small shopping bag with the logo printed on the outside, holding it out to Jack by the handles. "Enjoy and accept my true congratulations, love birds!"

Cindy thanked her, deeply curious about all this, but trusting Jack to let things unfold in his time.

Which he did, but it took a while. They walked hand in hand to Kaneo, a gorgeous Mediterranean restaurant and bar they had grown to love.

Inside, it was busy but without a wait for a lunch table. The hostess recognized them and snagged them a two-top near the window. As they sat, Cindy looked around the lovely restaurant, inhaling the scents of basil and rosemary that permeated the place.

A young server with an earnest smile and a mop of curls brought hot bread and a cheery greeting.

"Happy almost-Christmas," he practically sang. "We've got a spiced carrot soup today that will make you believe in miracles."

"Two?" Jack said, glancing at Cindy for agreement.

"Yes, please. Soup sounds amazing."

As they waited for their order, the box sat on the table between them, silent and bright.

Cindy chewed her lip. "If I shake it, will it jingle?"

"Probably not the best idea," Jack said, amused. "You like that store."

"I *love* that store. It's the same and not the same. Like us."

"Well, the floorboards creak like my bones," he said with a laugh, then slid the box closer. "Open it. Happy almost wedding day."

Sucking in a soft breath, she lifted the box from the bag. Her fingers went a little clumsy around the twine, oddly excited.

"I don't have a gift for you," she said.

"You are the gift, Cinnie."

She chuckled at the name only he dared to use—and she loved it.

Pulling at the wooden snowflake, she slid it free and set it beside her water glass. "I'll hang that on the lodge tree."

The paper gave with a whisper. Inside was a sturdy keepsake box, matte and white, the lid printed with a faint pattern of snow. She lifted the lid.

Nestled in more tissue lay a snow globe cupped in a ring of pearl-tinted glass, the base brushed silver like winter light.

The scene inside was an entire world. A tiny bride stood beneath an arch—*the* trellis—her dress a suggestion of satin and lace, her hair—exactly Cindy's pale blond—lifted by a hint of breeze. The groom faced her, head tipped a fraction as though saying...I do.

Behind them, the artist layered pine boughs and a faint outline of the lodge wall, strung with wee lights.

The ground was a crisp sweep of snow, unmarred except for two overlapping heart-shaped prints where they stood.

"Oh, Jack. This is..." Cindy's throat thickened and tears blurred her vision as she turned the globe to read the small plaque on the base, bearing their names and the upcoming wedding date. "This is exquisite."

She couldn't speak for a second. The world condensed to the heavy glass in her hands as she admired the miniature arched trellis that matched the one she would fight to keep in the Starling Room.

"I'm speechless," she admitted.

Every detail was perfect, from the way the bride's chin looked stubborn and soft at once to how the groom reached for her, as if to put on a ring.

"Go on," Jack suggested. "Give them a little weather."

Cindy tipped the globe gently. Snow lifted like quiet applause, slow and suspended, then tumbled down around the couple, clinging to the arch. The trellis—carved in the same pattern that Owen Starling himself had used—became a lace of frost.

"How did you do this?" she asked in awe.

"Fritz did it, and I gave him pictures."

"It's perfect." Her voice broke. "It's *us*. It's the trellis, and I know I've made such a fuss about that stupid thing, and—" Her throat grew thick. "I could cry just looking at it."

"Don't." He reached across the table, palm up. "It's here forever, where no influencer could boss it away."

She squeezed his fingers. The earlier conversation about MJ and Matt floated at the edge of her thoughts—how life could be both steadfast and uncertain—and then drifted off like the last flakes settling at the base of the trellis.

Right now, right here, the world had narrowed to this table, this man, this tiny scene of them made into a snow globe.

"I'm going to put it in my new office," she whispered. "As a reminder of what's really important. Who is really important."

"Us," he corrected, lifting the tissue and box to fold it neatly.

"I love it," she said, running her finger over the glass with deep, deep joy. Then she looked across the table. "And I love you. Thank you for this gift. Someday, long after we're gone, I hope Nicole has this in her home and gives it to a daughter of her own."

His face almost crumpled. "Now you're going to make me cry. Let's get through our wedding first before I fall apart as the father of the bride."

She beamed. "That's going to be fun, isn't it?"

"Yes." He smiled, deepening the lines at the corners of his eyes. "I love you, Cindy."

"I love you, too."

The soups arrived in heavy white bowls, fragrant and velvet smooth. Cindy took a spoonful and sighed. "Whoa, the kid wasn't exaggerating."

Jack tore a corner of bread and dunked it. "So, what

do we do after lunch? Hooky is only real if you spend the day and do something wild."

"Okay, Ferris Bueller."

He laughed, then his eyes sparked. "Let's hit the ice rink!"

"Oh, yes," she agreed. "Red's tale of ice woe made me want to get out there again."

They ate with gusto and excitement for the next adventure, sharing easy conversation about this town and their past and a future so bright, Jack said—naturally—he had to wear shades.

When the dishes were cleared and the bill paid, neither of them was in a hurry to stand.

Cindy shook the globe once more, just a gentle flick of her wrist, and watched the flakes rise and fall again.

"I'm going to treasure it," she said. "Not just the globe. This. *Us.* The lunch, the surprise, the way you still make everything feel like we're thirty and not sixty."

"Wait until you ice skate," Jack joked. "You'll feel every one of those years."

On their way out, she slid her arm around his waist and looked up at him. "You know what I'm excited about?" she asked.

"The wedding? Christmas? A new year as husband and wife?"

"Yes," she said on a laugh. "All of it, the *future.* For years I've felt like I didn't really have one. Yes, I had the business, and Nicole will marry and have kids, but it was all...alone. All me. You've changed that, Jack. You've made me a 'we' again and..." Her vision blurred. "I'm so grateful and happy to have you back."

"I am so honored to be half of your we." He kissed her lips lightly and drew back. "But let's go easy on the ice. We don't need broken hips on our wedding day."

Laughing, they stopped at the car to put the snow globe away, then spent the rest of the afternoon spinning and sliding and, yes, falling. In love and on the ice.

Cindy simply couldn't remember ever being this happy.

Chapter Eleven

Benny

The metal door of the ice-skating rink's snack bar squeaked as Benny and Red trudged in, helmets under their arms, skates clomping awkwardly across the rubber mats. Their cheeks were red from the cold, and Benny's nose was running, but his grin was huge. He'd nailed his toy toss, and Red hadn't fallen once during practice, so a solid victory.

They snagged the closest bench so Red didn't wobble right to the floor. Benny helped him get out of his skates and then got their shoes from the locker.

"You hungry?" Red asked. "Because I smell buttered popcorn and hot chocolate, which have no right being together but pretty much seems like heaven right now."

Benny nodded enthusiastically. "Throw in a soft pretzel, Grandpa?"

"Oh, child, you know me too well." Red pulled out his wallet and handed Benny a twenty. "I'll get a table."

Benny scampered to the counter, bought the treats, and turned around holding a cardboard tray, scanning the tables for—

Oh, wow. Olivia had watched the rehearsal? He'd

seen Aunt Cindy and Uncle Jack, who'd taken a skate break to cheer them on, but not Olivia.

But there she was, at a table with Grandpa, yammering away. Not that Benny would call it *yammering*, but Red Starling sure would.

He headed to the table and set down the cardboard tray. "I didn't get you anything," he said to Olivia. "But do you want half of the pretzel?"

"No, thank you," she said, flipping back one of her braids, which were like dark, curly spaghetti that was somehow neat and wild at the same time. "I'm here for business, not pleasure."

Benny straightened his glasses as he slid into one of the other chairs, bracing himself for whatever she was up to now.

He picked up his pretzel, pulling it apart to share with Grandpa, ready for the first warm and salty bite.

Olivia slipped out of her puffer jacket, mittens dangling from the sleeves as she tossed it on the empty chair like she'd been invited for a long stay.

"What's your business?" Grandpa asked, regarding her with a mix of amusement and fear—rightfully so— over the rim of his cup of hot chocolate.

Reaching into her jacket pocket, Olivia snapped out a piece of paper with color-coded graphs. Oh, no. When she color coded, she was not fooling around.

"I've been doing research," she announced, flattening the sheet on the table. "Real, peer-reviewed, scientific research."

Red snorted into his coffee. "That's what you two

said before the vinegar-and-baking-soda volcano flooded my garage."

"That was *experimentation*," Olivia corrected primly, shooting a look at Benny. "This is data. We were still learning, right, Benny?"

They were last spring when they'd been paired by the teacher for a project. Olivia had been "the new kid" at his school that semester, but they'd met over winter break at a dog training camp.

Ever since, she'd been Benny's best friend, even though sometimes she made him crazy. They laughed more than they fought, and both loved the same books, movies, and, usually, experiments.

Then this whole dumb thing with her dad and his mom started and it changed everything because he felt like he was doing something Mom wouldn't like. But Olivia was so...forceful.

Olivia's eyes gleamed. "And what we're learning now is romantic success factors."

He nearly choked. "Olivia! I told you—"

"Hear me out," she said, raising a hand for silence. "Tomorrow night, your mom and my dad are building that gingerbread house together for Mistletoe on Main, right?"

He nodded, *hating* where this was going.

"This is our big opportunity," she said.

"We had our big opportunity," he replied. "We made it happen by negotiating with the Eleanor lady."

"Selling my soul and dignity in the process," Red chimed in as he dipped his pretzel in mustard.

Olivia plowed on, leaning in to make her point. "We cannot waste what I am now calling Operation Mistletoe Phase Two: The Scientific Method of Love."

The changing operation names mystified him almost as much as the girl who made them all up.

"Come on!" Benny complained. "Phase One probably cost me the cell phone I want for Christmas. You won't be happy until there's coal in my stocking!"

She tsked, unfazed by his fears. "Nobody really does coal, Benny. It's old English folklore."

Grandpa leaned back, that amusement in his eyes deepening. "Well, young lady, you should know that Benny's mom has made it perfectly clear that she does not want you messing with her personal life."

Benny almost hugged him. "That's right, so—"

"No one is *messing* with anything," Olivia said, brushing off the warning. "I promise! All we're going to do is test a few very simple hypotheses, Mr. Starling. We're dipping our toes into chemistry and human physiology."

"In other words," Benny said, "*meddling.*"

"We are examining the effects of certain outside criteria on the chemistry of the brain that makes a person think they are in..."

"Don't say it," Benny ground out. "Do not say—"

"Love." She grinned at him, then at Red. "It's all very scientific. And no one is going to get hurt, I promise."

Benny dropped his head into his hands. "Olivia, you can't make people fall in love. That's...that's..." He turned to Red. "Isn't it illegal?"

"I don't know about illegal," his great-grandfather said, eyeing Olivia like he'd never seen a specimen quite like her. "But it's certainly...ambitious."

"Don't encourage her, Grandpa."

She flicked her fingers like Benny was a fly. "He knows genius when he sees it, and this, my friends, is the work of a mastermind."

"Look, Olivia, I know you're smart, but a master—"

"It's from ChatGPT," she interjected. "Who *is* a mastermind."

"Chat...Jeep-tea?" Red scowled. "Who in tarnation is he?"

"Oh, mine's a female," she quipped. "I call her *Le Chat*"—she drew the word out and pronounced it weird—"which is French for cat, so how cute is that? Anyway, to answer your question, Mr. Starling, it's an AI program—artificial intelligence. The program helps people solve problems, like math or coding or romance."

"We're not allowed to use it in school," Benny said. "That tells you it should be off limits in the rest of life, too."

Red just shook his head. "Kiddo, if you need a computer for romance, you're doing something wrong."

"Not if the romance is a problem and Chat can solve the problem." She feverishly tapped her finger on the paper like a woodpecker on a tree trunk. "Here are my top ten ChatGPT-approved, scientifically backed ways to increase human affection in winter environments."

Benny groaned, already knowing he was going to hate these ideas. Or his mother would.

Olivia sat up straight and put the paper in front of her as if she were giving a speech to the class.

"Number one: in controlled temperature environments, people are more affectionate when they're warm, which I think the bakery kitchen will be, so check that one off. We do want to keep it exactly two point three degrees warmer than usual."

Red frowned. "Two point three? Why not two point four?"

"It would mess with the variables," Olivia said solemnly. "Number two: apparently, vanilla scent increases oxytocin production. So, let's strategically spill a bottle of it before they start working."

"All bakeries smell like vanilla," Benny said. "We don't have to waste my mom's very expensive Madagascar vanilla bean extract." He shuddered to think how she'd feel about that.

Olivia tipped her head in concession, giving him hope he could talk her out of this madness. "I can snag some from my dad's shop."

Or not.

He threw a look at Red, hoping for some backup, but he was more invested in his pretzel, listening as he ate.

"Next is strategic seat placement during the g-bread house assembly," she continued.

"Strategic...seat?"

She gave Benny the same look he got when he couldn't figure out a math problem as fast as she could, which was rare but did happen. "Eye contact must be encouraged and, if possible, constant," she explained.

"Why?" Benny asked.

She sucked in a surprised breath. "Do the words dopamine, adrenaline, cortisol, and endorphins mean nothing to you?"

"Sounds like a law firm I'd never hire," Red chimed in.

She laughed, her eyes bright as she looked at Benny. "You're so lucky to have such a funny grandfather."

"Great-grandfather," he corrected.

"Well, that's redundant," she said, giving Red a sweet smile. "But my point stands. Listen." She snapped the paper and read, "'Within seconds of locking eyes with someone attractive, key regions of the brain light up. Ventral tegmental area and nucleus accumbens release dopamine, the feel-good neurotransmitter. The amygdala processes emotional salience—'"

"What's that?" Benny asked.

"I don't know, but I think grownups do."

"Don't be so sure," Red mumbled.

"Anyway, it makes them 'hyperaware' of each other," she said. "The nervous system kicks in, and the bonding chemistry goes through the roof with feelings of closeness and—get this—a sense of *melting*."

"That's 'cause the temperature is two point three degrees too warm," Red said, cracking Benny up enough that they had to high-five.

"I get that you two think this is amusing," Olivia said. "But I, for one, am serious. That means we arrange every-thing so they are sitting directly across from each other at a prep table. Chairs with no escape routes. Also, music is critical, but slow Christmas songs only on the playlist, which I will handle. Slow jingles equal romance, high-tempo jingles equal chaos."

Benny curled his lip. "This whole thing is chaos."

"Now here's one to consider—adrenaline association. If they experience danger together, they'll confuse adrenaline with attraction. So I'm thinking we let something burn in one of the ovens, set off the smoke alarm—"

"No!" Benny and Red spoke at exactly the same time.

"We've set off alarms before," his great-grandfather said.

"I know." Olivia grinned. "I was there and have the Paws & Pals Winter Camp Talent Contest winning trophy to prove it." She looked from one to the other. "All right, never let it be said that I can't compromise. We'll bag the adrenaline. But not the chocolate and strawberries," she said.

"I'm kind of afraid to ask what that is," Benny said, feeling a smile.

"It's exactly what it sounds like. We must get some of your mom's chocolate on my dad's strawberries and...let nature do the rest."

"Do the rest of what?" Benny asked.

"Well, chocolate is made of phenylethylamine, which actually mimics the feeling of...liking someone. Chat calls it infatuation. Strawberries have something to do with vitality and...well, never mind. It works, that's all you need to know."

"Works with what?" Benny leaned in to demand. "If I'm going to be part of this nonsense, I need to know."

"It's something called an...aphro...something."

Red shifted uncomfortably. "Let's wrap this up, Madame Curie. We have to get home."

"Almost there," she said. "Chat said synchronized tasks are huge for building mutual attraction and optimal bonding, so we already covered that with the gingerbread house project. Oh, and, of course, mistletoe placement, but that'll happen the night of the festival, and the last usable suggestion is based on the light frequency theory. When Dad installs the fairy lights on the gingerbread house, we have to make sure they blink at the same rate as a human heartbeat."

"Eighty beats per minute," Benny said automatically.

Olivia smiled approvingly. "See? You're catching on."

"I'm catching the flu," he said dryly. "The Olivia strain."

She dropped her paper onto the table with a satisfied sigh. "So, are you in?"

"In what? Trouble? Yes, I'm going to be if we pull any of these stunts."

"Benny's mom was very specific, Olivia," Red said. "He is under strict orders not to meddle in grownups' personal lives."

"There you have it," Benny said, gesturing toward Red. "That'd be a big fat no, Olivia."

"We're not doing anything wrong!" she protested. "No one is getting hurt or tricked and you won't get in trouble, Benny. All we'll do is add a few outside elements to help what we both know is going to happen anyway."

"We know that?" Benny asked.

"My dad hasn't talked about anything but this project and your mom since they had that date the—"

"They went on a *date?*" Benny's voice rose with disbelief.

"Well, not exactly. Just coffee after the town meeting, but..." She lifted a shoulder. "I haven't heard him hum so much since the Steelers made the playoffs last year. So, yeah, we're just going to help Mother Nature."

"Except...Mother McBride is going to be mad at me, and I can feel that iPhone slipping out of my hand."

She just laughed. "I'll persuade my dad to bring me to your mom's shop, Benny. I'll have to leave Kat at home because that dog cannot be trusted in a bakery. But we can do homework together and"—her eyes flashed—"observe our subjects. I'll bring the vanilla. If you'd rather stay home, then I will conduct this experiment alone, but we're such a good team, Benny. Don't let me down."

She stood and smiled at Red, who looked the way he did when someone beat him at Monopoly and he never saw it coming. "You're quiet, Mr. Starling. Do you have anything you think we should consider?"

"I think you should consider trying to get your own TV show, young lady. I'd watch."

"Maybe I will," she said, folding her paper and stuffing it into her coat pocket when she bundled up to go back outside. "Gotta go back to Craving Clean. See you guys!"

With that, she blew out of the snack bar, leaving Red and Benny in stunned silence.

"Wow," his great-grandfather finally said. "She's...a force of nature."

"Exactly. A destructive, catastrophic, Christmas present-killing tsunami of bad ideas." Benny shook his head and gave a quizzical look. "What should I do, Grandpa? Let her do this alone or...supervise? I don't want Mom to get mad."

"No, you don't," Red agreed.

"But Olivia's right—it's not really anything that could hurt anyone. Plus, if I don't keep an eye on Olivia, she'll have the smoke alarm blaring, the vanilla extract flowing, and then they'll get locked in the storeroom having *eye contact*."

Red snorted. "Yeah, she needs supervision."

"Plus, she's my best friend," he said quietly. "Kids like us don't play sports or have a ton of friends. And Olivia is fun. I mean, she can drive me crazy, but she's fun."

Red took a long sip of coffee and eyed him. "You know, Benny, if her plans work out, you two could end up as siblings."

He felt a smile pull. "I think it would be cool to have a sister," he said. "And..." He let out a heavy sigh. "A dad."

Red's shoulders dropped as though they carried a little too much weight. "I get that."

"So, should I help her?"

"Yup." He put down the cup. "You do what a brother does and keep her out of trouble."

It might get him *in* trouble, but he knew it was the

right thing to do for his friend. And, hopefully, for his mom.

Chapter Twelve

The front lights of Sugarfall were dimmed to a cozy glow, the cases polished to mirrors, the chalkboard menu wiped clean except for a single snowflake. Olivia had drawn that while Benny helped Marshall transport a partially made gingerbread house across the street.

Gracie never dreamed Benny would want to spend the evening here instead of at home with Red, but he'd insisted that he and Olivia could do homework while their parents worked on their own collaboration.

Honestly, Gracie was thrilled the kids were here. They added a level of excitement and had made the whole project more fun.

The initial setup of the house—which still needed an official name on the display entry card that sat on the counter next to them—had gone well. The only mishap was a spilled bottle of inexpensive vanilla extract that Gracie had no idea was even in her kitchen. Benny had accidentally dropped it, giving the air a slightly cloying sweet scent.

Once the whole structure was built, Marshall and Gracie started the decorating phase, which they'd been doing for well over an hour now, settled into a comfortable rhythm. In the front of the bakery, the kids were talking and laughing more than writing essays or doing math problems.

That had Marshall and Gracie joking about how even their little overachievers had "winter break-itis" and could barely concentrate on these last few days of school.

Olivia had made a Christmas playlist that Benny uploaded to the bakery sound system, filling the place with holiday music. Olivia's choices had a surprisingly slow beat that actually relaxed Gracie as she concentrated on framing her doors in red licorice.

As she worked, the world narrowed to the hush of parchment paper crackling under her forearms and the clean, rhythmic squeak of a metal bowl turning against the counter.

Directly across from her, Marshall sat on a baker's stool that Benny had kindly set up for him. He wore an old Pittsburgh Steelers sweatshirt and jeans and piped a bead of royal icing—sweetened with honey and stiffened with whey—along the seam of their combo-structure's roof, his handsome features drawn in concentration.

He hummed under his breath—not to the music on the speakers, but something soft from his chest, a steady, almost holy melody. Every time he glanced up to check alignment, the overhead light caught his eyes, and the color reminded her of so many things she loved, like caramelized brown sugar, maybe, or a dark chocolate ganache.

Something warm and sweet and tempting.

Between them, the gingerbread replica of Sugarfall

and Craving Clean rose and came to life, two separate buildings that had yet to be joined.

"So how should we do that?" Marshall asked as they paused their work to consider the baking and engineering challenge.

"How should you do what?" Olivia asked, appearing in the kitchen with Benny as if they had been hovering outside—were they listening to the conversation?

Probably, given the fact that they'd orchestrated this whole *group* project.

"We need to connect the two structures," Marshall told them, waving the kids in. "Ideas are welcome."

"Sure," Olivia said. "Can we steal some strawberries and dip them in chocolate?"

A frown pulled as Marshall regarded her. "You don't like strawberries, Liv. You said they make your throat itch."

"Benny wants some," she said. "And you two might like them, too."

Gracie pointed to the walk-in fridge. "There's some chocolate on the first shelf that's easy to melt in the microwave, Olivia. And a basket of fresh strawberries. Help yourself."

"Will you eat a few?" Olivia asked.

"Of course," Gracie assured her. "But we need two giant brains to help us figure this out."

The kids came closer and examined the work, oohing and ahhing over the marshmallow snowdrifts banked against pastel candy bricks on the Sugarfall side. Olivia gushed over the gumdrop topiaries marching down a walkway crushed from candy canes into rose-white gravel.

Of course, Benny—always wanting to be fair—complimented Marshall on his almond-flour walls in perfect plumb lines, sunflower-seed shingles with realistic texture, and the protein bar "pillars" flanking a fondant door stamped with CC in neat block letters.

"In order to submit this as an entry in Mistletoe on Main and get the PR benefit and foot traffic, we have to have one structure," Marshall explained, pointing to the card Eleanor Locke had left in his mailbox earlier that day. "I was thinking a connector piece that we cover in icing—"

"Icing?" Olivia leaned into Gracie with a smile, whispering, "That's what my dad calls whipped coconut cream with monk fruit."

Gracie laughed. "We can just use good old fondant and sugar."

"What about a bridge?" Benny suggested.

They all looked at him, interested.

"Full disclosure," he added, "I'm trying to write a book report on *The Wind in the Willows*. The bridges over the river are symbolic, at least according to my research—"

"Yes, Benny!" Olivia gasped. "That's exactly—oh, perfect! A bridge is a...a *connection*!" She cooed the word, drawing it out with just a little too much meaning.

"Between different worlds," Benny added. "And businesses."

"And *people*." Olivia clapped. "Definitely a bridge.

And while you make one, I'll get those chocolate-covered strawberries ready. C'mon, Benny. Help me so these two can...create the connection."

Gracie bit back a smile, looking over the prep table at Marshall. Did he see what they were doing or—

"How can we make a bridge?" he asked, far more pragmatic than his little girl.

"Umm...with spun sugar? It will look like ice."

"Beautiful, but..." He lifted his brows. "Spun sugar is not in my wheelhouse."

"Don't worry—it's at the center of mine," she assured him, standing up. "I just need to reduce some sugar, water, and corn syrup—"

He flinched. "Corn syrup? Really?"

She just laughed and waved him closer to the stove. "Come on, I'll teach you. And can I just say how great it is to have a couple of geniuses for kids?"

"It makes life interesting," he agreed, standing to join her. "You sure there's no substitute for that corn syrup?"

"Not in my kitchen, Mr. Hampton."

Laughing, he followed her to the stove. As she brought out the ingredients to pour in a pan, Gracie marveled again at how comfortable she was in his company. Had she ever spent this much one-on-one time with a man and not blushed every second? He just made her feel so at ease.

"Didn't you learn how to spin sugar in pastry school?" she asked.

"Pastry school?" He gave a noisy snort. "Self-taught, my dear. Well, mom-taught. But she was as good as any pastry chef. The health stuff came from years with trainers, but the baking? All credit to Germaine Lydia Hampton."

"Really?" As she placed the pan on the heat, she looked up at him. "Tell me more about her."

He leaned a hip against the stove, crossing his arms, a glint in his eyes. "My mother..." he started, a smile growing. "Well, she's definitely where Olivia gets her...everything. Brains, relentless determination, and a spirit that I believe will conquer anyone and anything."

Gracie laughed, fully agreeing with that take on Olivia. "All beautiful character traits, Marshall."

"Amen."

"You mom had time to bake, work in a hospital, and be a waitress?" She marveled at what that had to be like, especially raising a son alone in the inner city.

"She never slept, I swear," he replied. "We had a tiny kitchen in an apartment but most days, if you closed your eyes, you'd think you were in a bakery as big and beautiful as this one."

She smiled at the compliment, stirring the sugar and syrup mix, looking for the pale amber color she needed as he talked.

"Sweet and savory, she could make it," he said. "Pound cakes with the tops cracked just right. Cornbread in a five-dollar cast-iron skillet she called the family heirloom. And, yes, I still have it. She seasoned that sucker to glossy perfection and I hope to give it to Olivia."

She smiled at that.

"She always sang while she baked," he added, getting her to look up.

"You hum."

"I guess I do and probably the same songs—'Come Thou Fount' and 'Go Down, Moses.' To me, baking is deeply attached to Sundays after church where my mother was the loudest sister in the choir belting out gospel music." He laughed, but she sensed a bit of an ache in the sound.

"She used to tell me baking was an extension of a good Sunday service," he continued, clearly lost in thought. "She said people showed up mad or sad or tired, and you fed 'em—scripture or sweets—and their hearts softened enough to hear whatever they needed to hear. About grace. About being kind. About trying again tomorrow. Then she'd quote her favorite book."

"The Bible?" she guessed.

"In general, yes. Matthew in particular. I think I had the Sermon on the Mount memorized before I knew my ABCs."

From across the kitchen, the kids laughed and a spoon scraped against a metal bowl, but Gracie hardly heard it, mesmerized by Marshall's voice and words.

"She sounds wonderful..." Her voice broke, and she swallowed at a sudden tightness in her throat. "Like the very best kind of mother."

His eyes flickered with warmth. "I hope I can be half the single parent Germaine was."

The words hit Gracie hard. "What happened to her?" she asked, as gently as possible.

"Heart." He exhaled. "We'd moved her close to us, and I thought we had more time."

"I'm sorry." The words were a small thing to offer next to a three-year absence, but it was sincere. "My dad died six years ago, and I miss him every day."

"Big loss for you," he said. "And Benny, though he talks about...Red? Your grandfather, I guess."

She nodded. "Red is his great-grandfather and the strongest male figure in his life."

He was quiet for a moment, then shifted on his feet and gestured to the pan. "It's bubbling."

She looked down at the boiling sugar and syrup, then checked her watch as she pulled it off the heat. "We're good. Eight more minutes, then we have to work fast. Spun sugar gets tricky."

They watched the mix for a second, then she asked, "Did you bake when you played football?"

"I kept baking the whole time I was in the NFL," he said, chuckling. "I had a reputation as the guy who fed people and prayed with them if they wanted it."

For some reason, that painted the most beautiful image in her head—this big strong man bringing pie and prayers to the locker room. "Nothing wrong with strong faith," she mused.

"That's part of who I am," he said simply. "In fact, when I retired from the NFL, I considered going to Divinity School."

She drew back, definitely surprised by this. "*Pastor Marshall?*"

"Come on, now," he joked. "It's believable. I did officiate a wedding last summer."

"You did?"

He nodded, proud. "One of my offensive coaches for the Steelers wanted to get married out here in Park City, and his fiancée liked the way I talked about commitment, so...they asked me. I was so honored," he added with a smile. "I took the online course to get certified and licensed in Utah, met with the pastor at my church, and I married them way up on a cliff in Alta last July. It was incredible."

"It sounds like it," she said, slipping a spoon into the sugar to test the consistency. "Well, Pastor, are you ready to make a spun-sugar bridge?"

"That's it? We ready to spin?"

"Yep. Let's build a bridge." She led him back to the table, where they prepared the parchment surface.

The kids came over with their chocolate-covered strawberries to watch. As they started, Olivia disappeared for a bit back to the front while Gracie showed them all how to spin and pull.

As the sugar hardened, Benny and Marshall sketched out a bridge and she started to lift and drag the sugar threads, carefully turning to shape them.

She let the sticky strands drift from her special whisk, each one catching the pendant light before settling in a glistening arc that bridged the gap between their storefronts.

"There's no way that's going to be a bridge," Marshall said, mesmerized by the process.

"It'll take some time," she whispered, giving the sugar her full attention. "And it does seem impossible at first. But you'll see."

Across from her, Marshall watched with open appreciation, giving her a jolt of satisfaction.

"You make that look easy," he said. "So graceful and artistic."

And...there was the blush. But it didn't burn or make her want to hide her face. In fact, she didn't even look down as she felt her pulse quicken.

Not because of a girlish crush, though. This time, what she felt was...deeper than that. Attraction? Yes. But even more.

Admiration. Respect. And something that made her whole body ache in a way she hadn't felt in a long, long time.

Finally, they had a bridge that stretched from a candy-covered roof to one made of almond flour, the hardened crystal glistening like an ice sculpture that joined their two worlds.

"Perfect," he said in a soft, low voice.

She looked up and her breath caught. He wasn't looking at the bridge. He was looking right at her, right into her soul. For a moment, she froze and felt her knees grow a little weak.

"Thank you," she managed.

He stepped back, blinking. "And I better look for some lights," he said quickly.

"I have them," Benny said, surprising Gracie, who had totally forgotten he was there.

"You do?" Marshall seemed just as surprised—like the two of them had been in their own little world.

"My great-grandpa found some LED lights with a special flash," Benny said. "They match the human heart rate, so people...will...love..." He glanced around. "Where'd Olivia go?"

"I'm right here."

Gracie turned at the tight note in Olivia's voice as she came back into the kitchen, clutching her backpack to her chest.

"You okay, Bug?" Marshall asked, frowning, as he must have heard the same thing.

"Yeah, yeah, I, um..." She swallowed, looking deeply uncomfortable. "I need to talk to Miss Gracie alone."

"Of course," Gracie said, already setting down her whisk to lead her into the office. "Come on, sweetheart. We'll be right back," she called to Marshall and Benny.

"We'll be making the windows glow," Marshall said, trying to sound light but Gracie saw his gaze track his daughter as she crossed the kitchen. Once again, she felt a wash of respect for how much he cared about this little girl.

Who definitely didn't seem like herself.

Gracie ushered her into the office, half bracing for a conspirator's grin, or some new scheme for her not-so-subtle matchmaking. Maybe Gracie should tell her to relax—her little setup was a success. At least on Gracie's end it was.

But the minute her office door clicked softly behind

them, Olivia's face crumpled and all the confident sparkle slid off like frosting on still-warm cake.

"I think I—" The rest dissolved into a rush of tears. "I think I got my period."

"Oh, honey," Gracie said, every maternal instinct snapping into place. She took a step and pulled the girl into her arms. Every inch of Olivia's long, lean body trembled, like a little scared deer. "You're okay. You're completely okay."

"I know what's happening," Olivia groaned into her shoulder. "I read the book, and there were videos, and I even made a kit, and I understand the shedding of the uterine lining."

Of course she did, Gracie thought, adding a squeeze so she didn't laugh at something only eleven-year-old Olivia Hampton would say.

"That doesn't make the first one any easier," Gracie said.

"And I left everything I need at home because who knew when this would happen?"

"The worst possible time," Gracie said wryly. "You can count on that."

She gave a weak smile. "I didn't want to tell Dad, and I thought about asking him to take me home but then I'd have to tell him and he's..."

"Not a woman," Gracie finished for her.

"I just...don't have anything."

"You have me," Gracie said simply. "And my private bathroom. And my entire stash of emergency everything, because life happens." She smoothed a braid over Olivia's shoulder and walked her to the small powder room in the back. "Bottom shelf of the cabinet. Use whatever you need. Take your time."

Olivia nodded, grateful eyes big. "Thank you."

When the door clicked shut, Gracie stood with her hand flat on the bathroom door, feeling the weight of this moment.

She remembered her own first time—how her mother's hands had been steady and sure, how they'd sat on the edge of the tub and laughed because laughter beat fear every time. When it was all over and they went back into the kitchen, MJ had placed a square of chocolate in Gracie's palm and said, "For your iron," and winked.

Gracie still didn't know if that was true. But she'd felt so loved.

She walked to the mini fridge, poured a cold cup of water, and pulled open her desk drawer for her secret Godiva stash.

The bathroom door opened a few minutes later, and Olivia stepped out, cheeks blotchy but chin higher. She'd washed her face. She'd smoothed her braids with determination. She was still a child, but one who'd stepped across a line she couldn't uncross.

"You okay?" Gracie asked.

Olivia nodded, then shook her head, then nodded again, laughing at her obvious wobble.

"I'm...yeah. I think so. It's just—" She made a helpless motion with her hand, looking very small and very brave. "I know it's natural and happens to everyone, but it's still big."

"It is," Gracie agreed, handing over the water and chocolate. "Take a minute. Then you can decide if you want to go out there or if you want to sit with me and talk. Either is fine."

Olivia took a sip and then a tiny bite of chocolate like it might explode. "You keep chocolate in the office of a bakery?" she asked. "Seems redundant."

Gracie chuckled not only at the idea, but at the fact that her bright little boy had certainly met his match with his best friend.

"I don't think any woman's desk should be without emergency chocolate."

Olivia let out a whimper as she finished the square. "You are *so* different from my dad," she murmured.

"And yet, here we are...building bridges."

Olivia smiled at that, then shyly stepped forward and put her arms around Gracie's waist again, offering a surprisingly fierce hug.

"Thank you," she said into Gracie's sweater. "Please don't tell my dad I cried. I guess I can figure out a way to tell him the rest."

"Any tears are between us girls," Gracie promised, rubbing her back.

They stood like that until Olivia blew out a breath and squared her shoulders. "Okay. I'm good."

"You're amazing," Gracie said. "We better go back and help the boys with those lights. Benny's definitely a big believer in 'more is better' and 'too many is perfect.'"

"As long as they beat at the right pace," Olivia said,

the comment confusing Gracie as they walked back into the kitchen.

There, she saw Marshall working furiously, on his knees, threading lights under the gingerbread structure—it could hardly be called a house—with Benny crawling around the floor looking for the outlet.

Marshall said something she didn't catch and Benny cracked up, as if in that short amount of time they'd created an inside joke. The amount of time it took for her to step into Olivia's life and be an on-the-spot mother.

Gracie exhaled, nearly swaying at the impact of the unexpected moment of intimacy and family and closeness.

Marshall looked up and his gaze went straight to Olivia, scanning her face with that split-second parental inventory when something might be wrong with a child.

Gracie lingered behind Olivia, catching his eye with a small shake of her head, silently stopping any questions.

He got the message and instantly turned to Benny. "Did you get that clip through the loop, Ben?"

The lump rose in Gracie's throat before she could stop it, freakishly emotional as if *she* was the one who'd just gotten her first period. Why was this all hitting her so hard?

"Okay!" Benny called out. "Plugging in!"

The gingerbread creation woke like stage lights had come on. Marshall's side glowed a clean, crisp white that made the almond walls look like new snow. Gracie's faux storefront bloomed in warm amber, with little red sparkles around the windows.

Where the two halves met beneath the spun sugar arch, the colors mingled—white bleeding into gold until you couldn't tell where one ended and the other began.

The kids cheered, but Marshall just smiled across the kitchen at her.

"Would you look at that," he murmured, holding her gaze with one that could melt all the chocolate in this room. "They meet in the middle."

She waited for the inevitable blush, a nervous laugh, the shy girl instinct to look anywhere but in his eyes.

But none of that happened. Instead, Gracie smiled right back and let a whole different kind of warmth fill her chest. Behind him, Benny and Olivia were high-fiving and popping chocolate-covered strawberries.

The whole kitchen seemed to shift out of focus, everything blurred but the face of the man in front of her.

Marshall picked up the entry form for Mistletoe on Main, walking toward her, never taking his eyes from hers.

"We need to name this," he said softly, tapping the card against his knuckles.

Name...*this?*

Well, it wasn't a crush anymore. It wasn't an attraction. Sometime between making the foundation for that gingerbread building and spinning the sugar into a fragile but beautiful bridge, she'd left anything that meaningless behind.

Because Marshall Hampton wasn't just a good-looking guy who'd once played professional sports and happened to open a competing business. He wasn't merely a neighbor or the father of Benny's pal. He was...

Extraordinary and faithful, strong and intelligent, caring and loving and kind.

She tore her gaze from his and looked past him at the sparkly, spectacular, snowy delight that captured their personalities, their businesses, and their...relationship. *Whatever* it was.

"How about Sweet 'n' Clean?" she suggested.

He dropped his head back and laughed. "I love it."

And she, a little voice in her head whispered, could love *him*.

Chapter Thirteen

Cindy

The black SUV that pulled up to the lodge could have been carrying a head of state. Dominique stepped out first, wrapped in a snow-white belted coat, her eyes covered by sunglasses large enough to double as shields. Behind her, a young man in a beanie and a leather jacket hauled some bags and equipment, then a woman with a makeup bag strapped across her body like a medic kit emerged to scan the porch with a judgmental gaze.

"Hello, I'm Dominique Parrish," she announced, as though the name itself were trademarked. "You must be Candy."

"Cindy," she corrected, extending a gloved hand. "Cindy Kessler. Welcome to Snowberry Lodge. We're so thrilled you could—"

"Cute," Dominique interrupted, glancing up at the recently refurbished roof.

Cute? The roof was forty thousand dollars' worth of shingled perfection.

"Rustic without being *too* folksy," Dominique continued. "Could film well, depending on the light. Parker, get some shots before it clouds over. He's my cameraman and muscle. This is Sloane." She gestured toward the other woman, a petite brunette who couldn't be twenty-five, currently reading her phone. "She's makeup and brains. Keeps me organized, beautiful, and on time."

Sloane looked up and gave a smile that certainly didn't reach her eyes. Then she tapped the screen in her hand. "Speaking of," she said, "you have exactly two hours and forty-two minutes until we have to be at the Grand Hyatt, Dom. Make them count."

"Oh, is that where you're staying?" Cindy asked, fighting the punch of disappointment that they had chosen her nemesis hotel. Before Matt's extravagant gift, she'd lost so much business to the name-brand resort strategically situated near a Deer Valley lift line.

"No, we have a rental."

"Then...are you skiing or..."

Dominique threw her a look. "There's another bride having a small wedding there and the third is at a restaurant in town."

Cindy frowned, not sure she followed. "So, you'll be filming three weddings while you're here?"

"Oh, heavens, no," she scoffed and threw a look at Sloane. "We'd die! No, just one, but we're making the final decision after seeing all three."

For a moment, Cindy felt the blood rush out of her head. "You mean...you're not...definitely using Snow-berry Lodge?" There hadn't been any talk of competing for this honor.

"We just couldn't decide, so we narrowed it to three. An old-fashioned lodge, a modern hotel, and a chic restaurant." She gave a tight smile. "We'll pick the one that works best."

"Oh...I, uh, misunderstood," Cindy murmured, really not wanting any more stress and not loving "old-fashioned" as her descriptor. "I thought you'd—"

"There are so many options," Dominique said. "Who knew Park City was such a destination wedding spot?"

Cindy knew. She kept her chin up and gestured for them all to come inside. "My sister and co-owner has warm pastries and drinks for you. Cocoa or tea or—"

Dominique snorted. "You can't see it, but under this coat is a body that never ate a warm pastry. Just take me to the venue and let's get to work."

"I'll take one," Parker called out as he planted a stabilizer in the snow. "Pastry sounds dope."

Breezing by her, Dominique stepped up to the porch, flicking her fingers toward the adorable wooden snowman with a scarf MJ had knitted herself.

"Love that. A total cheesefest, but it could sell."

A...*cheesefest?*

Cindy shook off the insult and led them through the lodge to show them around.

Dominique whipped around the first floor during a tour she obviously didn't want to take. She managed a cursory wave to MJ, who stood at the ready with her scones and tea like the Queen herself had arrived.

"It's quaint," she announced when Cindy breathlessly finished.

Somehow "quaint" didn't sound complimentary.

"You haven't seen the property," Cindy said. "We have six cabins on twenty-five—"

"Where's the Starling Room?" Dominique demanded, whipping out of her coat and throwing it across a sofa.

"I was saving that for last."

"Don't save, Cindy," she said, giving a wrinkle-free frown that screamed of Botox. "Show. Stat. Come on, Sloane. I need your opinion."

Cindy nodded and led the way, leaving Parker with the pastries.

She opened the double doors with her breath caught in her chest, suddenly weak with how much she wanted to beat the competition.

Yes, this was stressful, but being featured by Aisle Files would fill up her venue faster, better, and more effectively than a year of brutally expensive advertising.

So this was cheaper and more efficient, but...

Two other venues?

She bit back a groan and tried to see the Starling Room through Dominique's oh-so-critical eye.

It was glorious! No one could call it *quaint*. Nicole had sprayed some sweet perfume to mimic flowers and Jack had put soft music on the speakers.

The glass walls framed the mountains like art, making the light wood floor gleam. They'd set up the chairs, had the flower stands in place, and all the drapes were open.

Dominique didn't even glance in the general direction of the spectacular view. Instead, she marched up the center aisle and stared at…oh, dear. The trellis.

Dominique's heels clicked once, twice, then stopped. "Cindy." She sounded like a disappointed parent. "I thought we talked about this."

Ready for it, Cindy squared her shoulders. "It's staying for my wedding. If others don't—"

"I'm not featuring any others, Cindy," she said sharply. "It's the wedding we are here to cover—*may* be here to cover—that matters to me. This is an *abomination* and it will have to go."

"But my fiancé—"

"Sloane? Thoughts?"

Yanked from her phone, the young woman blinked at the arch.

"It's brutal," she muttered. "Like being trapped in the Home Depot garden center."

Whoa, rough. "It's a family piece," Cindy said, digging for calm and all the rationale she'd practiced. "When you marry at a place like Snowberry Lodge, the beauty is in the history. This trellis arch was built by my grand—"

"It goes or we go." Dominique crossed her arms.

Cindy sucked in a soft breath.

"I'm sorry," Dominique added. "I have standards and they must be met."

"Well, we have standards, too."

They all spun around at the sound of Jack's voice. He stood in the doorway, in the white shirt and dark pants he wore under his sleigh ride costume, looking calm, cool, collected, and very handsome.

Here comes the cavalry, Cindy thought with a burst of affection.

But would his help cost them this opportunity? Her heart dropped to the floor at the thought of what a lose-lose situation she was in.

"And who are you?" Dominique asked with a surprising amount of interest.

"The groom," he said simply, walking forward. "I'm Jack Kessler, Cindy's fiancé."

"And ex-husband," Dominique said, proving that she *had* listened to "Candy" on that first phone call. "I can see why she'd want you back."

Wait. Was she *flirting* with Jack?

Dominique came closer and extended her hand. "I'm Dom, Jack. I hope you're going to use those nice muscles to move the eyesore."

He shook her hand, held her gaze for a second or two, then put an arm around Cindy. "That eyesore has been in Cindy's family for generations," he said. "It's symbolic of happy marriages and long-lasting unions."

Dominique lifted an eyebrow. "It's symbolic of hunting lodges and haunted forests." She sniffed and turned to Parker. "What do you think?"

He looked through a camera lens, still chewing a pastry. When he swallowed, he shook his head. "The lines fight the geometry of the room. Move it outside, maybe behind the glass as a backdrop. See? Problem solved."

Dominique took a deep breath and shuttered her eyes on the exhale. "Well, then, we'll just—"

"I'll move it," Jack said.

Cindy whipped around. "Jack! You can't—"

"Yes, he can," Dominique said. "Parker, set up for some B-roll shots. Sloane, get me powdered. Cindy, I want to see you on camera. And, Jack, darling, why are you standing there? Carry that monster out of my sight."

Cindy saw Jack breathe in hard enough to flare his nostrils, but he just flicked a brow in Dominique's direction and walked past her.

While Sloane got Dominique powdered, Cindy hustled to Jack.

"Honey, what are you doing?" she asked, stepping up to join him on the platform.

He turned. "Cameron's in the ski shed with Nicole. Can you get him over here?"

"Jack, the trellis...our good luck...you were so adamant."

His features softened as he looked at her. "MJ told me there are two other venues in the running."

"Yeah, I guess I thought it was a done deal, but..."

"You want this, Cindy."

"But you want the trellis."

He lifted a shoulder. "Not as much as I want you to be happy."

She pressed her fingers to her lips. "Jack."

"Really, it's fine. We'll do a champagne toast under it after the ceremony. It's fine, Cin."

She closed her eyes.

"You really want to fight her on this?" he asked.

"No, I really want to find the words to tell you how much I love you."

He smiled. "I love you, too. Now, get Cameron."

On a sigh, she turned, practically walking into Dominique, who arched one judgmental brow. "There's a lot to be said for a man like that," she muttered.

The comment surprised Cindy. "I know. He's awesome."

"He's a sexy silver fox who will photograph well," she said with a wink. "Big points for your cute little lodge."

Cindy forced a smile and walked away.

CINDY STOOD at the back of the Starling Room, peering out the window to glimpse the black SUV fishtail a little in the slush before righting itself and gliding down the long, pine-flanked drive.

Silence fell over the lodge like fresh snow. Not quiet —there was the hum of the heating system, the soft clink of mugs in the kitchen, a distant whinny from Copper after a sleigh full of people climbed off and headed inside.

But mostly, she sank into the sound of...no one named Dominique Parrish. That woman was—

"Hey." Jack's hand brushed Cindy's back. "I thought I'd find you here."

She turned to him, not surprised he'd found her. It

was like he had radar when she was upset. He leaned to kiss the top of her head, the way he always did when he could sense her composure was tearing at the seams.

"You okay?"

"No," she said, honest and light in the same breath. "Yes. I don't know."

"Pick one," he teased gently.

She turned to look around them, seeing the empty chairs squared into tidy rows, the sweep of glass gleaming around the mountains, the ghost of the trellis.

The platform looked naked without it. There was so much room suddenly—room for air, light, and doubt.

"I can't believe you moved it," she whispered, an ache pressing behind her sternum. "I know how much you wanted it there."

He shrugged, playing it off, but she felt the little ripple of unease under his calm. "Just did what had to be done."

"Still." Her voice caught. "Thank you."

MJ appeared in the doorway, cheeks pink from the kitchen's heat and the guests she'd just plied with cookies and cocoa.

"Did the royal motorcade leave?" she asked.

"Not one minute too soon," Jack said gravely.

MJ looked around with cautious hope, and her shoulders dropped at the sight of the empty platform. "So, the rumors are true."

Cindy braced for disappointment—MJ loved that trellis, too—but her sister's eyes grew soft and bright at once, and she nodded slowly.

"That was brave," she said, looking at Jack. "I know what it means."

"What it means," he said, with that same wave-it-off ease that didn't fool either of them, "is we're going to give the other two venues a run for their money. My girl doesn't like to lose." He punctuated that with a kiss on Cindy's nose. "And I love my girl. I gotta go cool down Copper."

With that, he slipped past MJ and out the door.

Cindy stood a moment longer, then exhaled and looked at MJ. "You doing okay?"

"Mm." MJ came all the way into the room and put an arm around Cindy, guiding her to the chairs. "It smells nice in here."

"The only thing she didn't want to change, MJ. Look at the drapes."

"Who closes off a view like that?" MJ asked with a face of pure disgust.

"Someone who thinks they should control lighting." Cindy shrugged. "It's easier than light time."

"Invented by us." MJ laughed and tightened her arm around Cindy. "You know something about Jack?"

"That he's wonderful?"

"Yes, that. But, whoa, that man loves you."

Cindy sighed, because sometimes she just couldn't believe how much. "It knocks me out."

"Please remember that this is your wedding week, little sister."

Cindy nodded, her heart a mix of gratitude and

nerves. "I know." Then she eyed MJ, catching something weird in her voice. "Everything okay with you?"

MJ didn't answer, but when she turned her face to Cindy, something had slipped. Like her optimism—bright, steady, unflappable—had a nick in it.

"I'm fine," MJ said, too quickly, then shook her head, laughing at herself. "No, I'm not. I'm being dramatic. I'll stop."

"Don't," Cindy said, taking both of MJ's hands, warm from the kitchen. "Please. Be dramatic with me."

MJ stared at their hands, her thumb smoothing across Cindy's knuckles. "He's not coming back, is he?" she asked, very softly.

The question darn near hollowed Cindy out.

"I don't know," she said, honest enough and kind as she could make it. "I don't know, MJ."

"I keep telling myself he's dealing with something. Maybe it's a big, noble, ridiculous mess and when he drags himself out of the tunnel, he'll come straight here and throw his arms around me and say, 'Oh, how I've missed you, Mary Jane.'"

Cindy's heart cracked from the words and the look of longing in MJ's eyes.

"And every time the front door opens, my heart...it just—" She pressed her hand to her chest. "It still jumps."

At the first row of chairs, they sat down like a couple of guests at someone else's wedding.

"I'm sixty-three," MJ said, her voice oddly matter-of-fact. "I know I'm not *old*-old. I'm lively. I can go up and down three flights of stairs without an ache and make breakfast for a full house of hungry guests. But sometimes, I feel like...is that all there is, Cin? Is this it?"

Cindy closed her eyes, knowing that feeling of isolation and disappointment so, so well. She had ten years of them after Jack left. How had she held on? What advice could she give her sister?

Of course, she knew the answer and hoped it would be enough.

"MJ," she said softly, "even if you never held a man's hand again, you have Gracie and Benny and Nicole and Red and me. And now Jack. You have family, which is everything you need."

She huffed out a breath, nodding before whispering, "I guess I got my hopes up."

"You were born with your hopes up," Cindy said. "It's the thing I love most about you."

"But I started...imagining." Her voice cracked. "I shouldn't have."

"Oh, MJ." Cindy slipped an arm around her and pulled her in. "You are so loved and needed and treasured. This whole world would be dimmer without you. And, honestly, if he doesn't know that, then..."

"I read his letter again last night," MJ admitted. "I kept rereading the line that said, 'When I come back, it'll be as a simple man who fixes pipes and wants to court a classy, gorgeous, good-hearted woman the way a proper gentleman should.'"

"Talk about romantic," Cindy said on a soft laugh.

"And then I dreamed about George."

"Oh, MJ. George would have loved the guy. Don't forget he gave us a million dollars!"

MJ lifted a hand, then let it fall. "I'd give it back to have what you and Jack have," she confessed. "Don't hate me for saying that."

Cindy squeezed her tight. "*Hate* you? I love you more than anything in the world. And I understand. And I want that love for you."

They sat awhile, shoulder to shoulder, silent for a long time. Then someone dinged the bell in the kitchen and the front door opened and they heard Jack and Nicole's laughter...and life moved on at Snowberry Lodge.

"Do you think that diva is going to pick us for her social media stuff?" MJ asked, always the one to slice a situation down to a few key words and nail it every time.

"I don't know. I hope so. But if not..."

"Cin?" Jack's voice echoed from the kitchen. "Where's the woman I'm going to marry and make happy for the rest of my life?"

Cindy winced at the comment, squeezing MJ a little hard.

"If not," MJ said, "you've already won your own lottery."

And all Cindy wanted to do was share some of those winnings, just like Matt Walker had said he wanted to do.

As they rose and walked out, Cindy closed her eyes

and prayed so hard that that man didn't break her sister's heart. Because if he did, she'd...

She'd pick up the pieces. That's what they'd always done for each other and that would never change.

Chapter Fourteen

Gracie

M istletoe on Main was already an astounding success, Gracie decided, making a mental note to give props to Eleanor Locke and her team for a new and fantastic holiday celebration in Park City.

It didn't hurt that the weather cooperated beautifully, with a whisper-light snow moving in at sunset after a day of sunshine and achingly blue Utah skies.

Now, flakes fluttered through the air like shaken glitter, each catching the golden glow of the streetlamps along Main Street, which was exclusive for pedestrians that day and night.

Down the festive and fully decorated street, brass instruments played a jaunty version of "Jingle Bells," and the smell of kettle corn and roasted chestnuts filled the air. Laughter spilled from bundled-up families sipping cocoa and cider as they wandered to each display outside the shops and restaurants.

Gracie stood beside "Sweet 'n' Clean"—the joint extravaganza that sat proudly in the middle of Main between their two bakeries.

Their whimsical creation had exceeded her highest hopes, perfectly blending her sugar-coated fantasy and his clean, modern sensibility. One side was pastel pink with candy shingles and spun-sugar icicles dripping from the roof. The other sleek was and architectural, with walls of almond-flour brick and cacao-bean trimmed windows.

In the center, where their styles met, the spun sugar bridge glistened in the light, drawing compliments and many pictures from admiring crowds.

Gracie snuggled into the fur collar of her winter jacket, her hands deep into her pockets as she watched people pose with her creation, then choose if they wanted to taste treats from the "sweet" or "clean" side.

Their assistant managers, Amanda for Sugarfall, and Roberto for Craving Clean, stood side by side at a table giving out samples in tiny tasting cups, laughing together at the friendly competition.

And wasn't that what this was? A friendly competition.

Gracie glanced a few feet away to where Marshall stood chatting with a young couple he knew from his church. His dark hair was hidden under a knit hat, his laugh deep and easy. As they all talked, Marshall stole a look to the side, directly at Gracie.

For two or three heartbeats, they held eye contact, sending a rush from her head to her toes. She felt a smile pull. He gave a secret wink.

Right then, it felt like all of Park City froze in a moment of anticipation and hope and promise.

Could Marshall feel the same things she did? Could he be as attracted to Gracie as she was to him?

Was it possible...

She tamped down the questions as Olivia popped up beside her, a glimmer of mischief in her beautiful eyes.

"I saw that," she whispered, leaning into Gracie.

"Saw what?" she replied, biting back a laugh. "That little kid who almost touched the spun sugar bridge? Thank you for saving the day."

Olivia giggled and tugged at the leash that held her border collie. "Just promise me one thing, Miss Gracie."

Gracie narrowed her eyes. "You scare me when you say that, Olivia."

She trilled another laugh. "When we go to see Benny and Red skate? You'll sit right where I put you."

Just then, Marshall sidled up to them. "What are you two scheming about?" he asked with a teasing smile.

"None of your beeswax," Olivia quipped, pulling her red cap over her eyes. "Oh, there's another dangerous five-year-old, ready to smash Sweet 'n' Clean!" She scampered over to the little boy like she was the museum curator and police officer all in one.

"I heard a rumor," Marshall said, leaning just close enough to torment Gracie when she met his impossibly dark gaze. "And it's not good."

"Another bakery coming to town?"

"Gah, I hope not," he said, sounding sincere. "I heard we're in the running to win the Gingerbread House contest."

"Oh, we'll win," she said confidently. "We are the parents of Olivia Hampton and Benedict McBride, neither of whom knows the meaning of the word lose."

She thought he'd laugh, but his expression grew somewhat serious as he considered what she said. Was it the kids or losing or...what?

"So, what's not good about winning the contest?" she asked.

"There's only one plaque," he said. "So, who'll get it?"

She felt a smile lift her lips, not because of the conversation but just...being near him. He had such a glow about him, such a deep light that drew her in. He made her feel good and hopeful just by existing.

How did he do that?

She had no idea, but she liked it. She liked him.

"I guess we'll share plaque custody," she said. "Like Benny and Olivia were supposed to do with the dog trophy that I understand has never left Olivia's bedroom."

He tsked. "She's greedy with her prizes."

"We can draw straws," she suggested. "Or set up a schedule."

"Or arm wrestle."

She laughed. "Like I have a shot against you, Number Twenty-Seven."

His eyes flickered with surprise at the admission that she'd gone to the trouble to look up his old jersey number. Oh, boy. So busted.

"And *there* it is," he said, dipping a millimeter closer.

"There's...what?" A truth bomb?

"That beautiful Gracie McBride blush that I never get tired of seeing."

She huffed out a half-laugh, half-grunt, touching her

gloved hands to her cheeks. "Even in thirty degrees, my cheeks give me away."

"I love it," he said, which only deepened the blush more. "It's like a little window into your thoughts and feelings."

"Oh, dear," she murmured.

"What? You don't want me to know your thoughts and feelings?"

"If you did, it would be..." She closed her eyes, no doubt scarlet by now.

He closed the space between them by putting his mouth next to her ear to whisper, "It would be game over?"

She bit her lip. "At least...a penalty."

"Are you really going to use football analogies? Because..." He put a hand on her shoulder, and she darn melted onto the snow-covered ground.

"Because you'll win?" she finished for him, her whole body humming with the flirtatious exchange.

"I'll lose...the thing I'm trying so hard to hang on to."

She searched his face.

He just tapped his chest with one finger, right over his heart. And Gracie was...yeah. She was done. Finished. *His.* Did he have any idea—

"Whoa!" Olivia cried out, making them both whip around. "Don't touch that bridge!"

Another little boy was instantly pulled back from the display by his mother, who apologized and reminded him not to touch.

"It's fine," Gracie assured the mom, waving off her

worries. "I'd be shocked if the bridge lasts the whole night."

"It'll last," Marshall said, putting a light hand on her back and adding a smile.

Olivia sighed in resignation and came closer. "I don't want it to break under my watch," she said.

"Then let's end your watch, young lady." Her father reached for her hand. "And let's walk around and see the other displays. Roberto will warn off wayward little kids."

From behind the table, Roberto gave a playful salute. "We got this, boss. Go enjoy the night."

Next to him, Amanda nodded. "By the way, 'sweet' is winning by a slim margin."

"Very slim," Roberto added, giving her a playful elbow as some more people came up to the table for samples.

A minute later, Gracie, Marshall, and Olivia meandered down the middle of Main Street, with Kat leading on her leash. They passed carolers in Victorian costumes singing under a string of twinkle lights, and a vendor dressed as an elf handing out paper cones of caramel corn.

Gracie's heart felt light, her cheeks still warm from the exchange with Marshall that couldn't be described as anything but romantic.

They walked like, well, a family, making her miss Benny with a sudden pang. They *could* be a family—Marshall, Gracie, Olivia, and Benny.

Could that happen? Could that dream actually happen?

Yes. She couldn't remember the last time she'd felt this *steady* with someone. Around most men, her nerves twisted into a tight knot—too much small talk, too much wondering if she was saying the wrong thing. But not now, not with Marshall.

They turned a corner, following the crowd streaming toward the rink. Olivia trotted ahead, her pom-pom hat bobbing, Kat sniffing happily at her boots.

"I see Benny and Red," she called, pointing toward the ice. "They're getting ready!"

Gracie smiled, catching sight of her son in his own elf costume—green tunic, red hat, socks with bells that hung over his skates. He was buzzing with energy, his glasses crooked under the hat, his cheeks rosy and merry.

Red sat on a bench, hunched over, looking the part of Grumpy Santa. In fact, he didn't even smile when Olivia called their names, but he gave a wave to her. Then his eyes lit when he saw Gracie and Marshall not far behind.

"I'll be back, Benny," Olivia called, then whipped around. "I reserved you two seats, so you must follow me, Dad and Miss Gracie."

They shared a look and a laugh.

"I refuse to apologize for her," Marshall joked. "She shall rule the world, and I just hope I'm around to see it."

"I hope I am, too," Gracie agreed, blowing a kiss for luck to Benny.

Olivia guided them to some temporary benches at the rink's edge, right beneath a giant cluster of lights and hanging candy canes. She'd used scarves and gloves to save three seats.

"Right here, you guys! You can see everything!" she called proudly.

"Perfect," Gracie agreed—and realized just how perfect when she noticed the giant mistletoe hanging above them. A few sections down, she spotted her mom with Cindy, Jack, Nicole, and Cameron.

Catching Nicole's eye, they waved to each other. Then her cousin gave a completely not subtle thumbs-up, then pointed over Gracie's head and mouthed, "Mistletoe!"

Maybe she mouthed it. Maybe she yelled it. The blood was rushing too noisily in Gracie's head when she turned to Marshall who, of course, saw the whole thing.

"Friend of yours?" he joked.

"My cousin. And mom. And aunt, uncle, future cousin-in-law, and...yeah. My clan."

He peered over her shoulder and gave a friendly wave. "Of course. I met them all last year. Want to go sit with them?"

She let out a sigh, sensing that he didn't want to move or make this a social event. "I like it here."

"Same." He put a light hand under her chin, guiding her face up so she had to look at what hung over their heads. "There's an old Christmas tradition about... *mistletoe*."

She laughed. "Yeah, I think I know it."

They stood there, face to face, the crowd and noise and snow fading into the background as they looked into each other's eyes. Gracie could feel his warmth through his coat, could smell the faint hint of his cologne.

"Can I watch from the railing?" Olivia called from somewhere behind Gracie. "Please, Dad? I want to be close!"

"Don't go too far," he replied, barely taking his gaze from Gracie.

She and Kat took off down the aisle, and then it was just the two of them—under the mistletoe, in the glow of the Christmas lights, the air alive with music and laughter and the sweetest tension.

"This night's kind of perfect, isn't it?" she murmured.

"It could be if..."

"If we follow...tradition." She pointed up, feeling her expression soften as if to give him the permission she could see him silently asking for.

He leaned in slowly, giving her time to move away if she wanted to. But she didn't. Not even close. The world faded to nothing but the warm curve of his mouth, the snowflakes clinging to his lashes, the faint sound of carols and bells in the distance.

When his lips brushed hers, everything disappeared —no noise, no nerves, no worries. Just him. Just them.

The kiss was slow and tender and wonderful.

When they finally eased back, her cheeks were warm, her eyes still closed. "Wow," she whispered.

"Yeah," he murmured. "Wow."

"Wow!" A sharp hand jabbed so hard at the back of Gracie's shoulder, she actually stumbled closer to Marshall.

Turning, she met the highly amused gaze of Eleanor Locke, who clutched a clipboard and wore a fur hat.

"Would you look at you two!"

Marshall gave an uncomfortable laugh, but Gracie felt way too much blood rush to her face, suddenly aware that Eleanor knew—

"I guess the scheming, matchmaking, and deal-brokering worked."

"Excuse me?" Marshall asked, his gaze flicking between Gracie and Eleanor.

Gracie opened her mouth to explain, but nothing came out.

"I say whatever gets a man to stand up, take charge, and notice, and you surely did that, Gracie McBride." She gave a sharp laugh and gave a lusty look to Marshall. "Quite a catch, too. Well done, you two!"

She added a really obnoxious wink and marched off, oblivious to the bomb she'd just detonated.

But Gracie could see the shock in Marshall's face, a hint of disbelief, a whisper of confusion, and a whole lot of...distrust.

"Wait. What?" he asked, stunned.

She opened her mouth, but *still* nothing came out. Her mind spun. Why hadn't she told him? She had no good reason, just general shyness and embarrassment.

"What does she mean?" he asked, an edge in his tone. "Scheming?"

"It's not what it sounds like," she managed. "It's—"

He studied her face, and she could see the realization dawning. "You...did this?"

"I didn't do anything, Marshall. I—"

"This was a setup? The co-baking thing? You... arranged this?"

"Not exactly..." Her voice wavered with the realization that he wasn't happy. He wasn't laughing or giving her a playful elbow or rolling his eyes over the cuteness of it. Not at all.

And that hurt.

"Unbelievable." He stepped back, shaking his head.

Was it so awful that she liked him and...did a little scheming? Not that she had. The kids had, but she'd gone along with it. "Please. It wasn't—"

He cut her off with a bitter laugh. "I thought it was real. Authentic. Turns out it was just...a scam."

A *scam*?

Before she could say another word, the crowd around them erupted in applause as the music swelled. The skating show had begun.

Gracie turned toward the rink, heart pounding, throat tight. "Can we talk after the show? Please?" she whispered.

Marshall's jaw clenched. He didn't answer but stared straight ahead.

On the ice, a troupe of girls came out in rows of three, the Christmas music sounding off-key and shrill to Gracie's ears.

Was it really that terrible of a thing to have done?

She watched the swirling skirts and spinning skaters, vaguely aware of Red and Benny on the sidelines waiting for their cue. It all blended together in a mess that made Gracie feel sad and sick and sorry she was here.

Glancing over to her right, she saw her family cheering the girls. Nicole and Cameron, arm in arm. Uncle Jack and Aunt Cindy, stealing a kiss. Even Mom looked happy as she clapped to the music and sang the words to a playful Christmas song.

Why wasn't Gracie over there with them? Safe behind her walls? She'd taken one step out of her comfort zone, and here she was, next to a man she could feel building his own barrier from her, brick by brick.

She'd known about his trust issues—his ex-wife's lies, the manipulation that had nearly cost him everything. And now, in the space of one careless comment, she'd become part of that same story. Her heart ached that he lumped her in with a woman who'd used him for fame, fortune, or marriage.

They both sat frozen and staring as the second number started, a medley of "Jingle Bell Rock" and "Rockin' Around the Christmas Tree." Two girls did a jitterbug routine and two more spun in gorgeous circles. Bells jangled and the crowd clapped and sang along.

A few skaters rolled a big tree to the center of the rink with the bag full of plush toys that Benny would throw. Gracie had come to the last rehearsal and knew every move by now, but the whole performance spiraled into a blur.

"It's really that awful?" she managed to ask in a raspy voice. "I mean, I didn't...hurt you."

Marshall closed his eyes and for a moment, she thought he was going to ignore the question.

"I just wanted to trust you."

"You can trust me!"

He turned to her, a world of pain in his eyes. "You know what hurts the most?"

She couldn't imagine. "What?"

"I let myself believe in you," he said. "After everything with Olivia's mom, I told myself I'd never get played again. And then you—"

"I wasn't *playing* you!" she insisted in a harsh whisper. "Marshall, listen to me. It was a silly plan, that's all! A way for us to spend time together—"

"Why not just tell me?" His voice was as sharp as a skate's blade. "Why make it a secret?"

"I..." Am shy? Was scared? Secretly wanted the kids' plan to work? None of her answers sounded right. "I don't know," she admitted on a sad sigh. "It wasn't very smart."

He shook his head, gaze locked on the ice. "Guess I should've known. Everyone always wants something. Fame, followers, the 'NFL connection.'"

Her breath caught. "You can't be serious," she said. "You can't think I care about anything like that."

"I don't know," he muttered. "I just feel...used."

Used? "I don't care about your past or your fame. I care about *you*."

He looked away, lips pressed tight. "I can't do this again, Gracie."

After thunderous applause, the notes of the next song started and every onlooker—except these two—started to sing.

You better watch out...you better not cry.

Too late, Gracie thought. The tears were already stinging her eyes.

Benny and Red skated onto the ice together and the place exploded as they slid toward the tree. Could anyone else see that Benny's whole reason for being on the ice was to support—literally and figuratively—his great-grandfather? That he loved the man so much he'd go out in front of the whole town and a couple hundred tourists dressed as an elf so Red wouldn't fall.

And so his mother *might* fall...in love.

"This was the deal," she said under her breath.

Marshall shot her a questioning look. "What...deal?"

She couldn't explain it here or try to toss blame on the kids. She just swallowed the lump in her throat, wishing she could be anywhere but where she was.

Then Benny started tossing plush toys and Red gave his grumpiest, "Ho-ho-ho," and waved his finger and mouthed, "I see you when you're sleeping!"

Benny glided beside him, working the crowd in the front row.

Gracie tried to focus, but her stomach churned. The music picked up. Doing his best Grumpy Santa, Red had his hand over his chest and frowned while Benny threw his arms wide, grinning like a loon.

The crowd laughed and cheered. For a moment, Gracie almost forgot the ache in her chest as she felt her lips move to the big crescendo...

Santa Claus is coming to...

Red stumbled and Benny swooped in to grab him, something she'd seen a few times in practice. Then Red went all the way down, sprawled on the ice, getting a sudden, "Oh!" from the crowd.

As that quieted, so did the music, and suddenly, Benny's high-pitched wail of terror cut through everything.

"Grandpa! Grandpa! Help! Someone help my grandpa! Please!"

There was a beat of silence, then the chaos of yelling and skates scraping and Gracie realizing that she was whimpering and crying out at the same time.

"Red! Benny! Oh, my God!" She shoved past Marshall as if nothing and no one could stop her from getting to the ice, but he snagged her hand.

"Be careful, Gracie!"

She ignored the warning and moved before her mind caught up. She shoved through the barrier, boots slipping on the edge of the ice.

"Red! Benny!"

Benny's sobs echoed through the cold air. "He's not moving!"

Cameron shot past her, calling out orders for someone to call 911 as he practically flew toward Red.

Cindy and MJ were running from the other side of the rink, Jack right behind them. Marshall was beside Gracie in an instant, steadying her as she stumbled onto the ice, heart hammering.

When she got to Benny, Red lay crumpled, his red hat fallen askew, his face as white as his beard and his eyes closed.

"I'm a medic!" Cameron yelled as he slid next to Red. "Everyone back up! Let me get his pulse!"

A *pulse?* This couldn't be happening.

She wrapped her arms around Benny, falling to the ice, oblivious of the cold as she hugged her vibrating, weeping son.

"It's okay, baby. It's going to be okay."

But she didn't know that. She didn't know anything except the sound of sirens in the distance and a glance at Marshall standing away from the circle, looking as stricken as Benny.

Christmas lights blurred, voices shouted, her breath came in ragged gasps. Somewhere, someone was saying they had a pulse. Somewhere else, she heard her mother sob.

But all Gracie could do was hold Benny and stare at her grandfather as more first responders arrived.

"Please," she whispered again. "Please, Red. We can't lose you."

And as the medics took over, Marshall's shadow loomed beside her, silent and stunned.

The night that had begun in magic and mistletoe shattered into a thousand jagged pieces of fear.

Chapter Fifteen

Was he dead? Was Grandpa gone? Another scream froze in Benny's throat, the words stuck there.

What have I done?

Everything around him blurred from tears and ice and a big white ball of terribleness in his heart.

"Grandpa!" Benny's voice cracked as he smashed his face against Mom's jacket, his whole body shaking with another sob.

He glanced over his shoulder when he heard Grandpa groan and try to bark at Cameron, who was talking in fast, calm words—pulse, pressure, transport—with the Santa jacket spread wide open as he did... medical things.

"If the ticker ain't broke, I'll freeze to death." Red rasped out the complaint, but the words lifted Benny's heart.

If he was complaining, he was alive.

"Come on, honey," Mom insisted, guiding him away from all the people and skaters and a bunch of firefighter guys with a stretcher.

They were taking Grandpa on a stretcher!

Lights kept flashing, and now some snow started falling, and all Benny could think was, *I did this. I made him do this.*

His mom's arms wrapped around him from behind, but Benny shoved forward, tears streaming down his cheeks. "I'm sorry! I'm so sorry, Grandpa! I didn't mean to—I just wanted—"

"Benny, sweetheart, stop," Mom said, her voice shaking, trying to pull him back. But he couldn't stop thinking about Red's face, the way it twisted up, the sound he made when he hit the ice, the way his eyes rolled back a little.

Feeling like he might throw up, Benny went slip-sliding over the ice with Mom, everyone parting to let them through. She kept murmuring things to make him feel better and telling him how everything would be fine, but Benny knew better.

Grandpa had a heart attack and could *die* because Benny'd insisted he skate in this show. It made him sick to even think about it.

"Gracie!" Marshall's voice cut through the noise, steady but loud. He was suddenly there, skating on his boots, Olivia at his side. "Let me take Benny. You go with your family to the hospital. I've got him."

Benny looked up at his mom, vaguely aware that he'd never seen her face that white. She was the same color as the ice, looking as terrified as he felt.

"No, no," she said. "He'll stay with us. With his family." She clutched at Benny again like she was scared to let him go. "I can't...leave him." She kept kissing

Benny's hair and he didn't care. He clung to her. "I can't."

"They're taking Red to Intermountain," Marshall said, very calmly. "Please go with your family and let me take care of Benny."

Mom straightened and looked at him. "I can't..."

"Yes, you can." He put his hands on her shoulders and for a minute, Benny thought he was going to hug her. "You don't know what's going to happen there, or what Benny..." He glanced at Benny. "You don't even know if they'll let children in the ER. Please trust me to take care of him and bring him to you the minute Red is in the clear. I'll treat him as if he were my own son."

As if he were my own son.

The words rang loud in Benny's ears, giving him an ache that felt like something was right and wrong at the same time. Like he wanted it so much but shouldn't dream that big. A dad like...Marshall Hampton.

"Oh, Benny." Mom folded again, hugging him. "What do you want to do, honey?"

"I, um..." He let out a wobbly breath. "I'm a little scared of the hospital."

Marshall instantly reached down and wrapped both Benny and Mom in his big arms, holding them tight.

"Come on, Gracie," he whispered. "I promise he'll be fine and you can concentrate on what the doctors say. Right, Ben?"

Benny nodded. "Mom, call Marshall when Grandpa...gets better, please? So I know."

"Gracie! Gracie!" Nicole and Uncle Jack came rushing to the side of the rink. "Is Benny okay?"

No, Benny thought. *I'm not okay. I'll never be okay until Grandpa is. I'll never—*

"All right, Benny." His mom put her hand on his cheek, drying tears. "You stay with Mr. Hampton and Olivia. I'm going with Uncle Jack to the hospital, and I will call the minute I can tell you he's fine. Marshall will take care of you."

He stood a little straighter and managed to nod but then clutched her jacket when his heart broke again. "Please don't let Grandpa die. Please. Please don't..." He couldn't finish. His throat shut tight, his voice gone.

"He's going to be fine. I promise." She turned away, fighting tears of her own. Then she looked up at Marshall. "I'm sor—"

"No, Gracie. I'm sorry. So sorry you're going through this. Take Benny off your mind. I'll have him with me in town and if he needs to come to our house tonight, he can. He's in good hands. I promise."

His words made Benny feel a little bit better, but then he looked past the man's big shoulder and saw tears pouring down Olivia's cheeks. Had he ever seen her cry? He didn't think she was capable of it.

For some reason, that made him want to be strong.

"I'll be okay, Mom," he said, forcing himself to stand up straighter. He swallowed, managed a breath, stole another look at Olivia. "You go and tell Grandpa I'm... I'm...that I love him."

She made a weird noise in her throat and hugged him

again, kissing him on the cheek. "He loves you so much, Benny-bean."

He smiled at the nickname only Grandpa used, needing to hear it more than he realized.

Uncle Jack hugged him, and Nicole, then they put their arms around Mom and took off, leaving Benny with a family that wasn't his.

"Let's go, Ben." Marshall scooped him up into a bear hug. He helped him get out of his skates while Olivia found his shoes and regular clothes. The whole time, Kat licked his mittens and put her snout in his lap because that border collie was smarter than anyone and knew something was wrong.

In fact, everything was wrong. A world without Red was...not what Benny wanted.

They ended up at Craving Clean, with Mr. Hampton—well, he told Benny to call him Marshall—sidestepping people and questions like the former professional running back he was. He took Benny, Olivia, and Kat back into his little office that was a lot like Mom's, only smaller.

Olivia brought in a blanket—pink, but he didn't care —and wrapped it around him while Marshall went out into the kitchen to get them...something.

"Kat has to stay in the office," Olivia told him, "or she'll go crazy if there's food on that kitchen counter."

He nodded, swiping his face, hoping he was done crying. His nose was stuffy, and his eyes burned like more tears could show up and slide down his cheeks any second.

"Benny, this was my fault." Her voice sounded raspy and like she might cry again, too. "I shouldn't have pushed for this."

"I pushed for it, too," he said, not sure why but he didn't want her to feel the guilt he felt. Nobody should feel like this. "It's not your fault."

"I feel so bad," she said, obviously not taking the pass he was giving her. "If anything happened to your great-grandfather..." Tears welled up. "I love him, too, you know. Not like you do, obviously, but he's funny and he's always so nice to me and...and..." A sob caught. "Benny, I'm so sorry."

"Why are you sorry?" Marshall asked as he walked back in, catching the end of that.

She looked up at him. "This was all my fault. I was pushing and pushing—"

"It's okay, Olivia," Benny said, quieting her. "Please don't cry. You know as well as I do that it's my fault."

"Then it's both our faults."

Marshall crouched down across from him, elbows resting on his knees as he looked from Benny to Olivia. His face looked tired and serious but not angry, not even a little.

"I think both of you need to tell me why you're taking the blame for this."

They both exhaled at the same time, sharing a look.

"It was my idea," Olivia said.

"And I went along with it," Benny added. "In fact, I think I was the one who told that lady we could make a deal."

"A *deal*?" Marshall asked as if the word really mattered to him.

"For Red to be Santa if..."

Once again, he and Olivia exchanged looks. Which one of them was going to tell him they were—

"If she would tell Gracie and me to make a gingerbread house together," Marshall finished, slowly nodding like Red when he finished the Sunday crossword puzzle. "Was this...your idea?"

"Mine." Benny and Olivia said the word at exactly the same time, in perfect unison. If smiling were possible right then, Benny might have grinned at her.

"So, it was a group effort," Marshall said. "And...your mom?" he asked Benny.

"Was pretty mad at me," he said. "When she found out what we did, she told me I shouldn't meddle and that she would tell you and call off the whole thing but then she didn't and I don't know why, so..."

"It was me, Dad," Olivia interjected into his breathless explanation. "Benny went along with it, but I just wanted you and Miss Gracie to...you know."

"Oh, I know," he said, with the slightest smile as he gave Benny a look. "Women," he whispered softly.

"Grandpa says you can't live with 'em and you can't bear life without 'em."

Marshall snorted softly. "Wise words from a great man."

Benny felt his face crumple. "He is! Which is why—"

Marshall put a hand over Benny's arm. "He's too tough to die, Ben. I promise you. And he's in good hands.

Your mom texted and said they already have him with a doctor in the ER and they're running tests. She said kids are allowed in the waiting area, so if you want to go, we can."

"Okay." His shoulders collapsed.

"But I need to know more about this scheme you two came up with."

"I made him watch *The Parent Trap*," Olivia started. "So..."

Her father smiled. "So you thought you could do a little matchmaking. And Red went along with that? Because I got the impression he didn't exactly relish skating as Santa."

Benny almost smiled, not sure what "relish" meant but getting the idea. "He hated it, but he did it for me."

"And you pushed him for me," Olivia said.

"And Gracie went along with it for..." Marshall closed his eyes and sighed before whispering, "Me."

Benny felt his chest hurt. "It was stupid," he said. "Making an old man skate was stupid and trying to get you and my mom... Well, that was stupid, too."

"And hopeful," Olivia said softly. "But Benny's right. It was pretty dumb, especially considering how smart we are."

Marshall moved his hand to cover hers. "You had good intentions, both of you. And Gracie had good... instincts. I'm the one who jumped to the wrong conclusions."

Benny wasn't sure what all that meant but nodded anyway.

Marshall didn't say anything for a minute.

Benny just sat there, quiet, waiting to find out what their punishment would be. The phone was history, that much he knew. But if anything happened to Grandpa—

"This isn't your fault, you two," Marshall finally said. "Not even close. And it sure wasn't Gracie...scheming." He winced as if he thought about something that hurt. "And Red wouldn't have done it if he didn't kind of want to."

"He does love attention," Benny said. "But not the kind with twenty firemen and an ambulance siren."

"Nobody likes that attention." Marshall's whole face looked like it hurt when he reached for Benny to hug him. "Do you know how to pray? Do you want me to pray for Red right now?"

He blinked. "You can, but I just want to know if he's okay. My mom said we could go, so can you take me there? I really want to see Red. He's like my dad and my grandpa and my best friend all mixed up together. What if...what if I never see him again?"

"You certainly will, but, yes, let's go. I'll pray quietly on the way there."

"Oh, what about Kat?" Benny asked. "Are dogs allowed in the hospital?"

Marshall smiled. "You know, Ben, it says a lot about a man who thinks about others—and dogs—at a time like this. We can take Kat and keep her on a leash. If they tell us she can't come in, then we can wait in the car. You need to be close to your family."

"Thank you, Mr....Marshall. Thank you for not being mad about...what we did."

"What *I* did," Olivia chimed in.

"Well, there's enough blame to go around," Marshall said. "Even some for me. Come on, team. Let's go. The hospital is less than five minutes from here."

Benny's heart lifted because they weren't in trouble... and Marshall called him part of the team.

Now if only Grandpa was okay.

A few minutes later, they piled into Marshall's truck, with Kat between Olivia and Benny in the back. The heater roared and snow hit the windshield under the streetlights as they drove.

Over Kat's head, Olivia looked at him. "It's gonna be okay, Benny," she whispered. "You'll see."

Benny wanted to believe her. He really did.

He stared out the window as the Christmassy town blurred by them, everything twinkling and happy and festive. Benny felt like the only person in the world who just had Christmas crack in half.

They pulled into a big parking lot next to the hospital and found a spot, but before they got out, Marshall tried texting Mom again, shaking his head.

"It's not going through," he said, staring at the phone. "That's good."

"Why is that good?" Benny asked.

"Maybe they don't have signal, and she just can't text to tell us Red is fine."

Clinging to that, Benny, Olivia, and Kat all climbed out of the back and walked toward the big gray stone and glass hospital rising out of the snow. The lights were bright, leading to a lobby that looked more like a ski lodge than a place for sick people.

Benny tried not to run, but he was ahead of the others when the automatic doors whooshed open and Mom walked out, looking at her phone.

"Mom!"

"Benny!"

They shot toward each other, her arms out. He collided with her like a cannonball, arms wrapping tight around her waist.

She fell to her knees on the pavement, hugging him so hard it almost hurt. "Oh, Benny," she breathed into his hair. "I've been trying to call. There's no signal inside—oh, sweetheart, he's okay. Grandpa is just fine."

Benny froze. "Really? He's not going to die?"

"Nope, he just had terrible heartburn," she said, laughing and crying all at once. "It wasn't a heart attack. The doctors said he scared ten years off all of us, but he's fine. He's getting a lecture about what he eats now..." She looked up, her gaze over Benny's head at Marshall, who'd just caught up. "Guess we'll send him to Craving Clean when he wants a cream puff."

For a second, Benny couldn't move. Couldn't breathe. And then everything inside him kind of fell apart when he realized Grandpa would be fine. Fighting another sob, he leaned into his mother as she slowly stood, still holding him.

"He's really okay?" Marshall asked.

"Are you sure?" Olivia demanded.

"Really." She nodded, smiling through tears and stroking Benny's hair like she did when she was really worked up about something. "He has zero indicators of a heart attack or any heart problems at all. They have a test they run that lets them immediately know if there's been a cardiac incident. This is definitely just severe heartburn."

"I told him not to eat that second hot dog before we skated," Benny muttered.

Marshall groaned. "I need to spend a week with that man and straighten him out."

Just then, more of Benny's family came out—Uncle Jack, Cameron, and Nicole—all rushing to hug Benny and share the good news.

"Where's Grandma?" Benny asked, looking around.

"She's with my mom, talking to the doctors," Nicole said, reaching down to straighten his glasses. "How are you doing, little dude?"

"I'm okay," he said.

Everyone started talking at once, hugging and laughing, and making Benny feel a little dizzy with relief.

Then he saw Marshall move toward his mom, kind of taking her to the side. He said something to her, and Mom looked up at him, not smiling.

He couldn't hear what she said, but Mom glanced at Benny, her eyes bright with more tears.

Olivia sidled up next to him, pushing him closer to eavesdrop.

"Gracie, I'm sorry," they heard Marshall say. "I was completely wrong and I'm sorry."

"What was he wrong about?" Olivia muttered.

"I don't know," Benny said, turning to her. "But I think we've caused enough trouble."

She started to smile, looking right past him. "Maybe. But check it out, Benny McBride. All that trouble... worked."

He turned just as Marshall and his mom hugged and—

"What?" he breathed, watching them...*oh*.

"And no mistletoe," Olivia said under her breath. "Just magic."

"And meddling," Benny murmured, looking away. He wasn't sure he wanted to see his mom do that, but still, he felt his whole face break into a smile. Olivia giggled and held her hand out for a secret low-five.

"Operation Mistletoe Madness for the win," she said, looking smug.

"You're crazy," he said.

"Oh, here he is!" Nicole called out, waving them all inside. "Red is here!"

The automatic doors opened again, and Grandma and Aunt Cindy came out pushing a wheelchair. And there was Grandpa. Pale, tired, still in his Santa pants and jacket.

"We have good news and better news!" Aunt Cindy announced, rolling him forward. "Dad is healthy and discharged and free to go home. And, not quite as important but still exciting, I just got a call that we were chosen by Aisle Files to be their featured wedding."

A noisy cheer went up, but not from Benny, who

couldn't possibly care less about the wedding stuff. All he could do was stare at Grandpa, who lifted his hand and crooked a finger to get Benny closer.

"C'mere, Benny-bean."

Benny bolted forward, flinging his arms around Red's middle so hard the chair rolled back an inch. "You scared me! You scared everybody!"

Red patted the back of Benny's head. "My ticker's fine, just a little rebellion from the second dog you told me not to eat."

"You should listen to me, Grandpa." Benny straightened and looked at the face of a man he loved more than anything in the world. "I told you hot dogs are dumb."

"Yeah, well," Red wheezed, smiling weakly, "you can't fix stupid."

Everybody laughed, and it sounded like music to Benny's ears.

Benny clung to Red's arm all the way to the parking lot. He kept glancing up, just to make sure his great-grandpa was still breathing, still cracking jokes, still *there*.

When they finally piled into the cars and trucks to head home, Benny leaned his head against the window and looked up at the night sky. The snow had stopped. The stars were back. Red was going to be fine.

He whispered, just loud enough for himself to hear, "Thank you."

Chapter Sixteen

The Aisle Files checklist was a map of sheer insanity.

Cindy stared at the unexpected email that popped up *three hours before the rehearsal dinner.*

Dominique said she'd stop by today for a quick walk-through, but she never showed, texting that she'd send an email with instructions instead and try to come by "later."

There was a later?

Cindy and Jack had done a rehearsal with Nicole and MJ, her only attendants, and Red, who was Jack's best man. In the days since the visit to the ER, her father had been quieter than usual, but back to himself. Benny, their ringbearer, was rarely more than a foot from the old man's side.

Jack had left for the airport to pick up his mom, and Cindy had been on her way to the empty cabin that MJ had designated as her "bridal suite" when she made the mistake of stopping in her office.

And there it was—the email from hell.

The subject line from Dominique glared at her in bold capital letters:

ABSOLUTE MUST-HAVES FOR VIRAL COVERAGE — FINAL!

Cindy groaned, letting her eyes skim the endless document. The bullet points had sub-bullets. The sub-bullets had footnotes. There were timestamps and suggested audio clips and little purple lightning bolt emojis calling out "trend moments."

The words blurred as Cindy blinked and read out loud.

"'Flat-lay of invitation suite with silk ribbon and vintage stamps (borrow if necessary)— include heirloom jewelry box for 'legacy' emotional resonance.'"

What did that even mean? Would a snow globe work? She glanced at the one on the shelf near her desk.

Then back to the email to read about an "opening shot" that described a pull-back reveal from the Starling Room to the mountain range during the golden-hour—oh, *now* she cared about light time just twenty-four hours before the ceremony—with "no guests in shot."

How could they do that? The guests would be there. She should just pile them into the Snowberry Lodge kitchen to wait for the *pull-back reveal*, whatever that was.

She scrolled some more, jaw tightening as she read about the "Get Ready With Me" TikTok moment with entire bridal party—there were two attendants!— including hair/makeup time lapse, trending audio (Dominique to choose from approved list).

With a mix of terror and a nervous laugh, she slid the cursor lower on the page to read about the champagne spray moment on porch or gazebo (weather permitting) with slow-mo toggle on for iPhone third angle.

"What language is she speaking?" Cindy muttered.

"The language of love, also known as a wedding cake." Gracie stood in her doorway, dressed in a beautiful black sheath with a silver scarf. "Would you like to see it? My mom is currently adoring it in the kitchen."

"Oh! Thank heavens!" Cindy stood and reached for her niece. "Finally, something about a wedding I understand. Cake."

"And it is one hundred percent the opposite of your first wedding cake," Gracie said. "As I promised Uncle Jack."

Cindy let out a soft laugh. "Jack's been so superstitious about doing things differently this time," she said. "So, no chocolate?"

"Vanilla and lemon, like you wanted," Gracie said, lifting her chin with pride. "With red flowers. It's gorgeous. Like, cry-a-little gorgeous. Come see."

"Let me—just—" She glanced back at the computer. The checklist sat there like a bad dream that would be waiting when she came back. "Speaking of superstitious—is it bad luck to hate someone the day before your wedding?"

"Only if it's the groom."

Laughing, Cindy followed her to the kitchen where MJ was indeed taking pictures and Nicole was practically dancing around a glorious three-tiered masterpiece.

Cindy's breath caught. The cake was a classic, frosted in a textured icing that looked like wind-swept snow. Tiny red roses spilled like a ribbon from the top tier to the bottom, tucked in with evergreen sprigs and little bits of cranberries that glowed like ornaments. It was beautiful and joyous and utterly perfect.

"Oh," Cindy whispered, hand to her mouth. "Gracie."

"Do you love it?" her niece asked, eyes sparkling. "I was so inspired knowing it was for you."

She wrapped an arm around Gracie. "It's a dream."

"Where do we keep it?" Nicole asked, circling like a cat who wanted to claim it. "Because I kind of want to stand guard until tomorrow."

"Let's put it in the dining room," Gracie said. "No one will be in there and it's better not to refrigerate it. The frosting will keep that texture and won't get sweaty. I have a special tent covering so no one will so much as breathe on it."

They took it to the large dining area where guests would soon fill the five small tables and enjoy breakfast before skiing when the lodge reopened. But today, as it had been for a year, this room was empty and the perfect place for her cake.

After Gracie had covered the cake and closed the dining room door, Cindy tried not to think about the email. She wanted to sink into the comfort of the kitchen with her sister, daughter, and niece...and forget about that checklist.

"Hey." MJ wound an arm around Cindy's waist. "You okay?"

Cindy tried to shrug and found herself shaking her head. The honesty rose so fast it made her lightheaded.

"I...don't know," she confessed on a sigh. "I'm thinking about the Aisle Files list. About trending audios and flat-lays and whether golden hour tomorrow will be cloudy and if Dominique is going to hate our chairs. But all I want to think about is my wedding."

Instantly, the three of them surrounded her, a contingent of emotional bodyguards, support and love at the ready.

Cindy let herself fall into the group hug. "I hate that I'm admitting this," she said, "but I'm more worried about getting this coverage than I am about...about marrying Jack."

Her throat closed around his name, not because it hurt, but because it meant everything.

"I know Aisle Files is our big break," she continued, the dam broken now. "Without this press, Snowberry Weddings may never make it onto the map. We've worked so hard, all of us. Dominique is...well, she's difficult, but she's giving us a shot. And it's...it's taking away from my big day, and I know it and I hate that I know it and I still feel like I have to do it."

Gracie reached for her hand and squeezed it so warmly Cindy felt it down to her toes. "It's a lot," Gracie said simply. "And you're right to feel like it's a lot."

MJ kissed her temple. "It's natural to want the business to thrive," she said. "But you are also allowed to say no to anything that steals your joy."

Nicole nodded. "We'll handle Dominique, Mom,"

she said with determination. "You're the bride, not the content provider."

But she was also the owner and manager of Snowberry Weddings. Somehow, she had to work while she got married. How had she put herself into such an awful corner?

"Tell us some of what's on the list," MJ said. "Maybe we can help."

"I wish." Cindy rolled her eyes heavenward and let out a tiny, strangled laugh. "It's fine. I'll get a few of the must-do's done and put off the rest. She rudely didn't show this afternoon and now I don't know when—or if—we can expect her tonight."

"Tonight is your dinner at High West Distillery," Gracie said. "You can't miss that!"

No, she couldn't.

"Let me go back and remind her that I'm the bride and she can figure this out tomorrow." But even as she blew a kiss and rushed back to her office, she was already thinking of a few things on that list she could squeeze in.

As she slid into her chair, the phone on her desk lit up with Dominique's name.

Or she could tell this human bulldozer to drive off a cliff.

Clearing her throat, she touched the speaker button. "Hello—"

"I'm waiting for your response."

Her back stiffened. "My rehearsal dinner is in a few hours," she said through gritted teeth. "My future—and former—mother-in-law is landing at the airport shortly.

My family is gathered and...I don't know what a slow-mo toggle is, so—"

The other woman laughed. "Bride panic. So natural. Listen, Cin, the crew needs to come by tonight—"

"We won't be here," Cindy said, fisting her hands. "We have a private room reserved for our dinner and—"

"All you have to do is gather a few things and we—"

Jack walked in, some snow dusting the shoulders of a tanned suede jacket.

"You're back early," she mouthed, then pointed to the phone on her desk. "Dominique."

He rolled his eyes and dropped into the guest chair, not looking any happier than she felt as the woman on the other end of the phone droned on and on.

"Listen, for our preproduction shots, I'll need the brides-maids' dresses laid out and I'd like a copy of your invitation, the RSVP card, and is the cake there yet? We could—"

Searching Jack's face, Cindy made a sudden decision. "Can you please hold, Dominique?"

"Well, I—"

Cindy cut her off and tapped the phone. "What's going on?" she asked Jack.

"Mom's plane got rerouted to Chicago. She'll get in tonight...at midnight."

"Oh, no. Poor Bertie."

He shrugged. "I'll pick her up after the dinner."

"I'll go with you," she said.

"It sounds like you'll be working...for Dominique."

Cindy closed her eyes. "Just let me get rid of her

somehow." She pressed the phone and took a breath. "Listen, Dom—"

"I know, I know," the woman interrupted. "You're freaking out. Time's tight on my end, so leave the lodge unlocked and I'll get into the venue. You go enjoy your little dinner thing. We'll get as much done without you as possible. Can do?"

It sounded like the out she desperately needed. "Yes," she said, not coming up with one reason why she had to be there.

"You can get to the rest of my list tomorrow morning. Bye!"

"Tomorrow morning?" Cindy spoke to the dead air, tears of frustration welling.

"What's the rest of her list?" Jack asked.

"You really don't want to know."

Without asking for permission, Jack turned her open laptop to read the screen.

His eyebrows climbed, then knit, then his mouth twitched, fighting a laugh. "Seventeen point five seconds?"

"I know," she whispered helplessly.

"And a neon sign?" he asked gently. "I thought we didn't do neon."

"We don't," she said. "Apparently, we do tomorrow." A sob caught in her throat. "Why am I doing this, Jack? Why am I letting this become about work and not us? It makes me feel like I can't do either one right—I'm a lousy manager and an even lousier bride. I just wanted this to be about our second chance and now...it's work. The one day I don't *want* to work!"

Tears dribbled down her cheeks as he took her hands in his much stronger, more capable ones.

He listened with the stillness that she loved so much about him, occasionally wiping her tears or squeezing her hands.

"Cin, you are an amazing businesswoman," he said quietly. "You built something beautiful, and you take care of people better than anyone I know. But we're getting married and we get to make the day what we want it to be. Not what somebody on the internet thinks will trend. Tell her to fly a kite and film that instead."

She wanted to say yes. She wanted to say yes and delete the list and run outside with him and laugh all the way to their rehearsal dinner. Instead, she stood to gather her thoughts, fast and sudden, her shoulder slamming into the floating shelf and rattling it—

Jack sucked in a breath just as she saw the snow globe teeter. On the edge of the shelf, her beautiful glass gift tumbled sideways, falling through the air.

Time stretched, thin as ice, and the globe moved in slow motion—the tiny bride and groom under the trellis frozen in their forever, glitter suspended around them like a promise about to shatter on the hardwood floor.

She and Jack lunged in the same instant, hands colliding in midair with a gasp. Their fingers wrapped the cold glass together. It shocked her—the weight, the suddenness, the simplicity of catching the treasured gift before it hit the floor.

They stood there, both breathing hard.

Cindy looked up at him, her eyes burning. The globe felt heavy and pure and...saved.

"Jack," she said, and her voice cracked on his name. "I almost wrecked it. I almost lost...everything. I almost did the same thing that broke us up the last time—putting work before us."

He looked at her, a storm of emotions in his dark eyes. "But you didn't. We caught it just in time."

Still holding the snow globe, they slowly straightened, as if the weight of the moment pressed on their shoulders.

Gently, like it was made of, well, glass, they set it on her desk.

"I'm sorry," she said, the words tumbling with the same speed as that near-miss. "I'm so sorry I got so wrapped up with Dominique and social media that I forgot what this is. I'm sorry about the trellis. I'm sorry I let her make me feel like we had to trade our story for a reel. It's our wedding, and I let it become her show. I'll call her now and cancel."

Jack's face softened, lines of worry and humor and love etching deeper in ways she wanted to memorize.

"I have a better idea."

She looked up at him. "What is it?"

"A surprise."

She inched back. "I almost just broke the last one you gave me."

"You won't break this one," he said. "Here's what I want you to do, okay? Leave this office right now and go to the cabin that MJ prepared for you. Do not stop in the kitchen, do not talk to anyone, do not look at your phone, your laptop, or anything but your mirror. Do whatever you want to do to get ready. Hair. Makeup. Your favorite dress and a glass of wine. Do not leave that cabin until I knock on the door."

She drew back, baffled and intrigued. "Then we'll go to dinner."

His mouth curved, and it was the smile he wore when he was up to something good. "Trust me."

She did. She always had.

CINDY STOOD before the mirror in the cabin, her reflection haloed by the soft glow of a single lamp. She admired the winter-white silk jumpsuit with pearl buttons that was somehow both bridal and festive. She smoothed her hair, the blond locks straightened by a flat iron she only brought out for the most important occasions.

Turning, she slipped into cream boots and glanced at the white faux fur coat she'd planned to wear into town for dinner.

But it was too early for dinner. Was Jack making her stay in this cabin so she didn't break his rules and try to... work?

She heard some noise outside—the sound of the

snowmobile and UTV, some voices, but she'd followed the rules, played her favorite music, sipped the wine MJ had put in the room, and spent the last hour preparing for...whatever Jack had in mind.

"Is my bride in there?" Jack called as he tapped on the cabin door.

"Yes," she answered on a giddy laugh, opening it to a cold rush of air. "Following my future husband's orders to..." Her words faded in the evening air as she took in the sight of him.

He filled the doorway in a dark suit and a gray wool overcoat, snow-dusted, with a dark suit underneath, a white shirt, and a thin black tie. His hair was wind-tossed, his smile easy. He looked like every Christmas movie hero she'd ever secretly swooned over.

"Wow." They said the word in perfect unison, making them laugh.

"You look beautiful," he said, reaching for her as he stepped inside.

"So do you," she sighed, taking the hug he offered, and the kiss. When she eased back, she gave him a dubious look. "We're early."

"Nope. We're right on time." He turned and lifted her coat, holding it for her to slip into.

She snagged her leather gloves and bag, her heart tapping with anticipation as they stepped outside and he offered his arm and led her to the sleigh, where Copper was harnessed and waiting.

"Ready for a ride?"

"Oh? A sleigh ride? I love that idea."

He helped her up to the front and joined her, the two of them nestling under a few fluffy blankets. Then he lifted the reins and clicked his tongue to set Copper into motion.

"Remember when he didn't want any part of this sleigh?" Cindy asked, cozying up next to him. "Now he's a pro."

"He thought he was done for the night," Jack said.

"But you want to take me..." She drew back, narrowing her eyes to guess. "To Bluebell Crossing where we had our first kiss."

He smiled. "I hate to be predictable, but yes."

"Not predictable." She slid her hand around the crook of his elbow, suddenly giddy. "Romantic and wonderful and exactly what I need the night before our wedding."

He leaned in and gave her a whiff of his oaky after-shave and a hint of pine that clung to him. "You smell like you've already been up in those wooded trails."

He just smiled at that as she settled deeper into the leather seats, tearing her attention from him to the woods bathed in yellow as the moon rose, and pinpoints of starlight appeared in the mountain sky.

Copper trotted along proudly, kicking up a little snow that swirled around the lanterns hanging from the sleigh to light their way.

The sleigh bells chimed with each of his steps, the big horse whinnying at the cold.

Cindy couldn't stop smiling.

When the trees opened onto the wide, snowy hill of Bluebell Crossing, Cindy sat up straighter at the sight of the lanterns—so many of them—that lined the route. And...there were people up here.

MJ and Nicole, Red and Benny, and—oh!

"Jack! The trellis?"

"Cameron and I have moved that thing so many times, it seems light to us now."

"Jack." She pressed a leather glove to her lips as the sleigh got closer to the gathering of the people she loved most in the whole world.

And a few extras.

"Is that Marshall Hampton and his little girl, Olivia?"

"Well, the pastor wasn't available on short notice."

"The..." Did he say *pastor?*

"But Gracie said Marshall is licensed to marry in the state of Utah. Olivia didn't have a sitter and..."

She let out a whimper. "Marry? *Now?*"

He brought Copper to a halt about fifty feet from the others, who all watched, quiet but smiling.

Turning to her, Jack looked into her eyes. "Right now, honey. This is official, legal, totally private, and...we will say our vows under the trellis that Owen Starling built. Please tell me you will marry me tonight. After that, I don't care what happens tomorrow, as long as you are my wife."

"Jack, this is...perfect."

"I thought so," he said simply. "Our first kiss, our

second marriage, our forever future. Don't worry, we'll still have tomorrow's wedding production—it'll be incredible. But this..." His voice caught, steadying again. "This one's for us."

Her throat tightened, tears blurring the lantern light. "Jack—"

He squeezed her hand. "I don't need a venue or light time or an audience. I just need you."

He jumped down first, then turned and held out his hand to her. "Come on. Everyone worked so hard to make this happen, and Benny has a playlist and...don't cry, Cin."

She blinked at tears as she carefully climbed down. "How can I not?"

He reached into the back of the sleigh and pulled out a bouquet of red and white roses, which must have been a signal to Benny, because just then, a portable speaker started playing soft classical music.

The small group parted to make room for them, and Jack offered his arm.

Cindy took a deep breath and took the flowers in one hand, and Jack's arm in the other.

Slowly they walked the short distance to the trellis, pausing to give MJ a kiss, and Nicole a hug. Cameron shook Jack's hand and Red squeezed Cindy with a murmur of love.

Gracie blew a kiss and Benny, standing next to Olivia, gave a thumbs-up.

Her family. Their family. She loved them all so much

that joy spilled through her chest until she couldn't contain it.

Laughter, music, wind in the pines, and soft words of encouragement filled the air, carrying Cindy forward to where Marshall stood holding what she knew was the Starling family Bible, welcoming them to a blessed and private ceremony.

"Marriage," he began gently, "isn't about the perfect photo, or the flawless day. It's about showing up for each other—again and again, day after day, year after year. And we are gathered here tonight to join Jack Kessler and Cindy Starling Kessler in a marriage that they vow will last forever. And this time?"

"It will," Jack whispered.

Cindy laughed through her tears. Jack grinned.

Marshall talked about forgiveness and patience, about choosing the same person and creating a history, about love and laughter and highs and lows.

Cindy heard the words, but all she could really do was look into the eyes of a man she'd loved since the first time he kissed her, right here on this mountain crossing, through decades and divorce and a do-over.

She belonged with Jack Kessler, and she would never leave him.

"Jack," Marshall said, "would you like to share your vows?"

Jack nodded, taking a deep breath. "Cindy. I've loved you since I first came to Snowberry Lodge and your father had the good sense to hire me to drive that sleigh." He glanced to his side. "Thanks, Red."

"One of my best decisions, son. And I'm famous for them."

Laughter rippled but quieted as Jack continued. "From that day to this, through raising a beautiful daughter, running the lodge, even the dark days when we parted, you were always my North Star. I will love you through whatever time we've got left—every morning coffee, every snowfall, every summer afternoon, every minute of every day. You're my home, Cinnie."

Tears streamed freely down her face.

Marshall smiled softly. "Cindy?"

She inhaled, her voice trembling. "Jack, you never fail to surprise and amaze me. You make me laugh and keep me calm and show me what matters in life. And if this moment isn't proof of that, I don't know what is." She glanced at her family, catching MJ's teary gaze. "I never stopped loving you, either, and I never will. We are in our sixth decade and somehow, we have a second chance at life and love. I can't wait to take it and never let go. I love you."

Jack brushed away a tear with his thumb, his eyes wet, too.

Suddenly, Benny scampered closer, holding out two boxes to Marshall. "The rings, sir."

Oh, they had *all* thought of everything! That much love nearly overwhelmed her.

Marshall delivered the traditional vows from memory —*to have and to hold, in sickness and in health, from this day forward*—and Jack and Cindy both delivered a heartfelt, "I do," and slipped wedding bands on each other's fingers.

"By the power vested in me," Marshall announced, voice full and sure, "by the great state of Utah and the Good Lord who is watching us, I now pronounce you husband and wife." He grinned. "Again. You may kiss your bride, and I hope you never stop."

The cheer that rose up from the little crowd echoed down to the canyon. Cindy threw her arms around Jack as he dipped her under the trellis and gave her the kiss of a lifetime.

After more hugs, a pop of champagne, and so many good wishes, they all piled into the sleigh and the snowmobile for a merry ride home as a fresh snow started to fall.

Cindy couldn't stop smiling, couldn't stop touching Jack's arm, his sleeve, the wedding band joined to her diamond engagement ring.

As they came over the last rise before the lodge, the chatter stopped as they saw the lights.

"Oh, goodness," Cindy muttered. "You Know Who and her crew are here."

"It's fine," Jack assured her. "You all talk to her while Nic and I get Copper into the stable. Then we'll head to town for a rehearsal dinner that just became a private reception."

Cindy, Gracie, and MJ climbed down and walked around to go straight into the Starling Room, which was blazing with bright lights.

Just as they stepped in through one of the French

doors, Dominique Parrish shot through the back door, covered—literally covered—in...in...

That wasn't *snow*. Oh, dear heavens, that was white frosting all over her green Chanel pantsuit. Which meant—

"The cake!" Gracie cried.

"The dogs!" MJ shrieked at the sound of Newt and Kat barking noisily.

"My wedding..." Cindy sighed, realizing at that moment she honestly didn't care.

Dominique marched forward, some icing falling from her collar. "Your *wedding* is the biggest mistake I ever made. No one was here to help us. I had to go looking for the cake. I had no idea there were two dogs sleeping in the kitchen and they scared the life out of me and..."

Gracie rushed off toward the dining room and MJ started to leave, but Cindy reached for her hand, wanting her sister's moral support for what was about to happen next.

"So we won't have a cake," the woman announced in her shrill voice. "And we won't have—"

"You," Cindy finished.

Dominique froze. "Excuse me?"

"First of all, Jack and I just got married in a private ceremony under the trellis on the very spot where we had our first kiss thirty years ago."

The other woman rolled her eyes, exasperated. "I could have used that footage, Cindy. Any chance we could—"

"There was no footage because there was no camera

because it wasn't done to impress, inspire, or entertain anyone."

Dominique drew back at the note in Cindy's voice and MJ stood a little straighter.

"It was a beautiful moment that will live forever in my memory."

She huffed a shuddering breath. "Fine. Now, can we get to the B-roll now that you're—"

"No." Cindy squeezed her sister's hand but kept her eyes on Dominique. "You're not covering our wedding ceremony or reception," she said. "I don't want Aisle Files here in any capacity. There will be no content for you, and you can...take the day off."

The other woman's jaw dropped. "Why don't you just close up shop now, Cindy, because without us, you will—"

"Succeed," MJ finished. "We have our own little social media guru, a few marketing geniuses in our family, and a history of hospitality and joy."

Cindy nodded in solidarity. "My sister's right. We don't need you to promote the venue but appreciate your interest."

For a long moment, the other woman stared at her, the look on her face saying she was not used to being turned down in any capacity. "Cindy, I'm sure we can—"

"Actually, we can't." Jack walked up behind Cindy and put his arm around her in a show of loving solidarity. "I think you heard my wife."

My wife.

Oh, it had been too long since Jack had called her

that. Unexpected tears sprung as she leaned into her husband and hero.

Dominique's gaze flitted over him. "Fine. I can still work with the bride at the Grand Hyatt. Parker!" She clapped her hands. "Sloane! Where are you?"

The cameraman slinked into the room, dragging a tripod. "We heard. We're packing up."

Her nostrils flared with her next breath.

"Can I get you some wet towels for that suit?" MJ asked, the picture of cordiality. "I wouldn't want the buttercream to stain."

"No, thank you. Goodbye." She slid her gaze to Cindy and then to Jack. "Best of luck to both of you."

With that, she pivoted and walked out, leaving them silent for a beat.

"Well," MJ said, "I guess the dogs didn't stay in the kitchen as planned."

Laughing, Cindy shook her head, shocked at how relieved she was. "Come on, let's go survey the damage."

MJ walked ahead, but Jack held tight, keeping Cindy back.

"You sure?" he asked, his brows lifting.

"Never been so sure of anything. Well, except that 'I do' I just said."

He kissed her lightly. "Good call, Mrs. Kessler."

Arm-in-arm, they headed through the back doors, around the kitchen, to find the entire family—and two very guilty dogs—in the dining room. The wedding cake was...demolished.

"The good news is there was no chocolate," Benny said, carefully wiping Sir Isaac Newton's face.

"And ChatGPT said that none of the ingredients Gracie used are toxic," Olivia added, also cleaning off her border collie. "I mean, unless you count sugar, which my father says is the devil's favorite spice."

Gracie, standing by what was left of the cake, didn't smile. Instead, she looked up at Cindy with true pain in her eyes.

"Aunt Cindy, I can make another one. I'd miss the dinner tonight, but—"

"No, you won't," Marshall said, stepping close to her. "*I* can make the cake. Olivia will help."

"I will!" the little girl chimed in. "I mean, if you don't mind almond flour and monk fruit."

"I can make a traditional, sugary cake," Marshall said. "It might not be as pretty, but I know how to make a cake Germaine Hampton-style. You'll love it. You go enjoy your family dinner."

Gracie smiled up at him, a spark so real between them that Cindy could feel it from across the room. "Are you sure?"

"I've got everything I need at my bakery."

"Except sugar," Olivia cracked.

Gracie hesitated, then sighed, reaching into the bag on her shoulder. "Here are the keys to Sugarfall," she said, handing them to him. "Everything you need is there and I'll come by after the dinner and help you with the decorations."

"Perfect. You ready to do a little baking, Bug?"

Olivia bounced beside him. "We'll make the best cake ever!"

Cindy felt her heart swell again—this family, always pulling together, always finding joy in the chaos.

They all stepped out into the snowy night hand in hand, dividing into groups for the cars, laughing and talking and replaying the best night ever—and they had only just begun.

Chapter Seventeen
MJ

The first wedding in the Starling Room was everything MJ had dreamed of since she was a very little girl. Two hours into the reception, the dinner plates had been cleared, the speeches made—Nicole had them all in tears—and the delicious last-minute cake had been cut and served along with an array of desserts from Sugarfall and Craving Clean.

All around MJ, family and friends from over the years floated by in sparkly dresses and handsome suits. They stopped to hug her, to congratulate the Starling family on the changes to the lodge, and to express their delight at Cindy and Jack's romantic reunion and second marriage.

Well, third, if you counted last night at Bluebell Crossing.

So why didn't MJ feel the soaring joy and high hopes that came with every wedding in general, and this extraordinary one in particular?

She certainly felt *something*. She'd spent the entire ceremony dabbing at the tears at the corners of her eyes, feeling her heart swell as she watched her sister marry the love of her life...again, and forever this time.

Plus, everything had gone off without a hitch—even with last night's wedding cake disaster and Cindy's courageous firing of that ridiculous woman and her crew. As Cindy and Jack had planned, they had an intimate affair with about forty-five guests, all who arrived at the perfect moment of their beloved "light time."

She smiled thinking about how easy the day had been, how calm and delighted Cindy was all day, and how happy...MJ *should* be.

But even a diehard optimist like MJ had to know when to face defeat, and she was pretty sure she was staring at that beast right now.

Well, too bad about Matt Walker, she thought, pushing up from her seat to force herself to walk the room and soak in the event. He'd made a promise and broke it. Unless she counted giving them a million dollars—which was surely worth more than a friendly flirtation with a nice man.

Wasn't it?

She sighed, picking up a champagne flute she had hardly touched to her lips in the last hour. She knew the answer to that nagging question but didn't want to admit it, even to herself.

She'd hoped. She'd hoped hard. And he would be here by now if he were coming back, so it was officially time to give up hope. And that, for Mary Jane McBride, was the most difficult thing of all.

Before starting her stroll, MJ looked down at the table, running her fingers across the lace overlay that covered the white tablecloth, steadying herself, digging for the cheer she wanted to show on this beautiful night.

Lifting her gaze, she focused on the things that mattered—and by things, she meant her wonderful family.

Starting with Benny, her one in a million grandson, zipping around the dance floor with his friend, Olivia, working the room with their iPhones. Yes, Christmas came early for Benny this morning, but they had good reason.

The two Gen-Zers—or was it something else now?—were filming every corner of the wedding, ready to blast social media with more love, authenticity, and appreciation for the Starling Room than that Dominique could have ever conjured up.

There was her precious daughter, Gracie, dancing with Marshall to a song about "every breath you take."

Next to her, Nicole bopped left and right with Cameron and Elise, always including her sweet future-sister-in-law without any hesitation about her wheelchair.

And of course, Cindy glowed brighter than the full moon, her joy palpable as she and Jack sang their old favorite songs to each other.

Red was perched on a sofa near the French doors, in conversation with Jack's mother, Bertie, who was about a hundred and ten pounds of sass and energy. She wasn't sure if her father was listening, planning his escape, or in shock, but he stared at the other woman with a typical Red Starling look of dismay.

MJ willed her heart to lighten up, enjoy this beautiful

night, count her ten million blessings and stop longing for something...*someone*...who wasn't showing up.

But who leaves a million dollars tied to a promise and doesn't keep it? What kind of man was he?

One she'd been thinking about for...345 days. Yes, she'd counted. Her calendar said what day of the year it was and he'd left on New Year's Eve. Not quite a year, but still...

When the song ended and another started, Gracie slipped away from Marshall and glided over to MJ, her long maroon dress fluttering around her frame.

"You okay, Mom?" she asked as she reached the table, a little breathless and flushed and...radiant. Now that was a sight that lifted this mother's heart. "You seem quiet tonight. I thought you'd be dancing to these '80s songs."

"I'm just overwhelmed with happiness, honey." She laughed softly, glancing around. "It's such a beautiful reception, isn't it?"

"What's beautiful is you," Gracie whispered.

"Oh, thanks," MJ said, waving off the compliment, although she had felt particularly elegant in her long navy dress with thin threads of gold sparkles. Plus, the professional makeup artist had been a fun confidence boost, too.

"I mean it," Gracie said. "And, yes, the reception is magical. I can officially relax now that the cake's been cut and served."

"And so good!" MJ exclaimed. "I practically had to tie Red down to stop him from getting seconds."

Gracie laughed. "For his own good. I'm just glad he's

feeling better and he's going to be fine. I don't think I've ever seen Benny that terrified."

"He'll be totally okay, thank the Lord. And you, my dear..." MJ wiggled her brows and jutted her chin in the direction of Marshall, who was now on the dance floor with his daughter. "Seem very...enamored."

Gracie's cheeks filled with that familiar pink flush that MJ had seen since this sweet girl had been born.

"I am enamored," she agreed. "And I think it's a two-way street."

"Marshall would be blind and crazy not to see all you offer," MJ said. "Even if you are competitors in business."

"Yeah..." Gracie sighed. "You know, I went over to Sugarfall last night after the dinner and helped decorate the cake."

"You didn't *help*—those were your tea roses."

"But it was his cake, and it was delicious." She lifted a brow. "Olivia had fallen asleep in one of the booths, and we talked until almost four in the morning."

"Oh? About..."

"About our lives, our kids, our businesses, our...feelings." Gracie slid a glance to the dance floor. "We're thinking about making some changes so we're not so competitive."

"Like what?" MJ asked.

"Well, to be honest, we started discussing the possibility of combining everything into one...entity."

"The bakeries? Or your lives?"

"Maybe both," she whispered. "There's definitely something there and I think it could be serious. We can start slow, but...yeah. There's potential for change and growth and...love."

"Gracie." She reached for her daughter's hands, squeezing. "He's an awesome man, and Olivia is a treasure."

"They fit in, right?" Gracie bit her lip. "It's early days, but the future looks bright."

For some reason, the words hit MJ's heart harder than she expected.

"So does yours," Gracie added.

"With the new lodge all upgraded? Cindy got more reservations today and we're looking full for January, so—"

"That's not what I meant, Mom."

MJ felt her face fall. "Honey, I'm done hoping."

"Hah!" Gracie gave a hearty laugh. "That has never—and will never —happen to you! Hope is your middle name!"

"Mom! Hey, Mom!"

They turned as Benny rushed over, sliding on the sleek bottoms of his dress shoes, his hair a mess, his glasses askew, his iPhone out and filming.

"Best moment of the wedding so far?" Benny asked, lifting the phone to Gracie's face. "We're going to edit a video survey."

Gracie laughed and stepped forward to answer, so MJ used the moment to step away, blowing a kiss. "I'm going to save—er, talk to my father. Come interview us later, Benny!"

She crossed the room and caught Red's eye, not

surprised when he stood fast, as if desperate for an excuse to escape Bertie Kessler. She was a *talker*.

"There's my girl," he said, extending a hand and giving a desperate look. "Did you come to dance with me?"

Bertie was up instantly. "Dancing is good, Red," she said. "I dance and do Zumba every week. You would love Zumba."

"Is that a type of pasta? 'Cause I love pasta."

"Clearly." Bertie lifted a drawn-on brow, which wrinkled her forehead. No surprise, she was eighty-five or eighty-six, MJ couldn't remember, but she did look and act much younger. "I'm going to spend the holidays getting Red to exercise," she announced.

MJ managed not to choke. "Well, he'll be busy as Santa Claus. It's his high season on the sleigh."

"We'll walk, stretch, and do a little chair yoga, Red," she continued, undaunted. "And if you need a Mrs. Claus, I bet I could find an outfit."

Oh, boy. "You're staying for a while then?" MJ asked the other woman.

"At least until the new year," she said, chumming up next to Red. "You know, I'm considered an unofficial personal trainer at the assisted-living home where I live—in the unassisted and independent wing, of course."

"Of course," MJ said.

"And I'm going to work my magic on this man who just nearly died."

"I didn't nearly die!" Red exclaimed. "It was heartburn."

"An early warning sign."

"Of impending doom," he deadpanned, looking at MJ.

The song switched to something slower, the first strains of Eric Clapton singing "You Look Wonderful Tonight," and MJ took the cue.

"Come on, Dad. It's not a wedding if we don't dance together. Mind if I steal him, Bertie?"

"Not at all. I'm here for weeks."

"God save me," her father muttered as they walked away.

"Dad, she's just trying to help."

"Help? She wants to build muscles I already donated to science."

Chuckling, MJ turned him and took his hand, assuming a dance position. "It couldn't hurt to get a few pounds off you, Dad."

He rolled his eyes. "Some people would call that elder abuse. And the woman could stand to eat a pretzel, you know. I've seen turkey carcasses with more meat on their bones."

But his eyes were bright and he was laughing, so MJ did, too.

"Are you enjoying the wedding, MJ?" he asked. "It really turned out nice."

"Yes, I am," she assured him. "My sister is happy and that makes me..." She swallowed the words that came up against her will. *Lonely. A little envious. Sad.* "Completely overjoyed."

Dad's bushy brows drew together. "You don't look overjoyed."

"*You* wear heels for four hours."

"Fair enough," he conceded, eyeing her. "Is it more than that?"

Why did she have to be as transparent as glass? "It's nothing, Dad."

"It's...Matt."

"No, it's not!" she insisted. "Why does everyone assume that? Why can't a woman be a little bittersweet on her sister's wedding day a year after some lottery-winning liar made a prom—"

"No, I mean, it's *Matt*."

"Dad, will you please—"

A hand touched her shoulder, warm, sure, and strong. "Mind if I cut in?"

She stumbled a little, the breath caught in her throat. Was she dreaming? Was this a fantasy? Could this be real?

"She's all yours, son." Her father took a few steps back, his eyes twinkling like he had his Santa suit on. "I think she's ready for...a better dancer."

Like it happened in slow motion, Graham Matthew Walker stepped into MJ's line of sight, filling every sense. He was taller than she remembered, even kinder looking. His moustache was still thick, his eyes still the color of cinnamon swirled in cream, and his chestnut hair had a few more silver strands.

But he was handsome, especially in a black suit with a crisp white shirt and tie.

"Mary Jane," he whispered, taking one hand and wrapping his arm around her waist. "This is the perfect song because you do look wonderful tonight."

Somehow, she managed to lift her open jaw. "Matt."

"As promised." He drew her an inch closer. "I contacted my attorney in town, and he mentioned this event and…" He lifted a shoulder. "I have a secret penchant for the dramatic."

"You think? Like a seven-figure check, a long letter, and a promise?"

He laughed, and she suddenly remembered how his laughter came from his chest and his whole big heart. "I like what you've done with the place, by the way."

"What *you've* done," she countered, still trying to drink in this perfect moment.

When had the attention of a man become perfection to her? About 345 days ago.

Matt smiled gently. "Did you think I wouldn't keep my promise?"

"No," she said, and meant it. "I didn't doubt you for one minute." Okay, maybe for a few seconds, but she kept that to herself.

He guided her in a slow circle, making her vaguely aware of more than a few eyes on them—including Benny and his ever-present phone.

"It's so good to see you." He breathed the words. "I've been dreaming about this moment. I must have thought about you a million times. A day."

She tried to tip her head, laugh at the compliment,

and pretend it was just flirtatious and meaningless. But she failed miserably.

"Same," she said instead. "And speaking of...a million."

"Don't." He shook his head.

"Don't thank you?"

"Don't make a deal of it. I've given all but a few away and I'm very happy." He gave her waist a squeeze. "Happier now."

And so was she.

"I'm sorry I showed up so late to this wedding, but I had to wait at the airport."

"Your flight was delayed?"

"Not mine." He glanced past her. "I brought someone with me."

"You did?" She wanted to turn and look but that would mean taking her eyes off him and she just didn't want to do that yet.

"My nephew asked to join me here for the holidays."

"I remember you talking about your nephew—Wade, right? Grew up in Alabama? Your sister's son?"

"What an amazing memory you have, MJ. Yes to all. I hope it's okay, he's trying to figure out his next move after finishing school. Any chance my old cabin is still available?"

"Every chance," she said. "And Wade is more than welcome. Is he—"

She glanced around. "We grabbed a hotel in town for tonight and he didn't want to crash the wedding." He slid into a slow grin. "But I sure did."

She let out a long, happy sigh. "Well, welcome to the Starling Room."

Glancing around with admiration in his eyes, he nodded. "Inspired. I'm so glad your girlhood dreams came true."

"They did. Thank you."

"You have any other dreams I can make come true, Mary Jane?"

"As a matter of fact," she whispered, letting her head fall slightly against his shoulder, the ache in her chest finally quieting. "You just did."

THE SNOWBERRY SAGA isn't over yet! Christmas is coming and there's another wedding on the horizon. Getting there won't be a simple sleigh ride, though. Gracie's journey to love hits an unexpected roadblock, Matt's nephew gives hope to someone who'd given up on a chance for love, MJ has to face down a ghost from the past, and Red and Benny...well, they take matters into their own hands one more time, which is always worth the return visit.

Come back to Snowberry Lodge for the New Year's Eve conclusion to Christmas in the Canyons!

Christmas in the Canyons by Hope Holloway and Cecelia Scott

Sleigh Bells in Park City
Snowfall in Park City
Mistletoe in Park City
Midnight in Park City

LOOKING for another Christmas collaboration from Hope Holloway and Cecelia Scott? Enjoy a Carolina Christmas, a charming, heartwarming holiday series that will whisk you away to a dreamy winter in the Blue Ridge mountains.

Carolina Christmas by Hope Holloway and Cecelia Scott

The Asheville Christmas Cabin
The Asheville Christmas Gift
The Asheville Christmas Wedding
The Asheville Christmas Tradition

If you're in the mood to bask in the sunshine of a gorgeous beach, fall in love with an unforgettable cast of characters, and get lost in stories you cannot put down... you've come to the right authors!

Other family saga beach reads by Hope Holloway and Cecelia Scott

Hope Holloway

Coconut Key

Shellseeker Beach

Seven Sisters

***

Cecelia Scott

Sweeney House

Young at Heart

***

Collaborations by Hope and Cecelia

Carolina Christmas

The Destin Diaries

***

Visit www.hopeholloway.com and www.ceceliascott.com for details about all of their books!

About The Authors

Hope Holloway is the author of charming, heartwarming women's fiction featuring unforgettable families and friends, and the emotional challenges they conquer. After more than twenty years in marketing, she launched a new career as an author of beach reads and feel-good fiction. A mother of two adult children, Hope and her husband of thirty years live in Florida. When not writing, she can be found walking the beach with her two rescue dogs, who beg her to include animals in every book. Visit her site at www.hopeholloway.com.

Cecelia Scott is an author of light, bright women's fiction that explores family dynamics, heartfelt romance, and the emotional challenges that women face at all ages and stages of life. Her debut series, Sweeney House, is set on the shores of Cocoa Beach, where she lived for more than twenty years. Her books capture the salt, sand, and spectacular skies of the area and reflect her firm belief that life deserves a happy ending, with enough drama and surprises to keep it interesting. Cece currently resides in north Florida with her husband and beloved kitty. Visit her site at www.ceceliascott.com